Collide

SUNRISE ISLAND BROTHERS 1
E. DAVIES

Copyright © 2023 by E. Davies.

All rights reserved. No part of this publication may be reproduced, distributed or transmitted in any form or by any means, including photocopying, recording, or other electronic or mechanical methods, without the prior written permission of the author, except in the case of brief quotations embodied in critical reviews and certain other noncommercial uses permitted by copyright law.

Publisher's Note: This is a work of fiction. Names, characters, places, and incidents are a product of the author's imagination. Locales and public names are sometimes used for atmospheric purposes. Any resemblance to actual people, living or dead, or to businesses, companies, events, institutions, or locales is completely coincidental.

Collide / E. Davies. – 1st ed.
ISBN: 978-1-912245-24-6

Collide

Prologue
FELIX

NOTHING CAN KILL MY MOOD TONIGHT.

I'm finally free. I have the apartment to myself. Hell, I've got my whole life ahead of me again, and I feel *amazing*.

No more angsting about what I'm doing wrong and how I can make my fiancé happy enough to say something nice about me. I'm done—with that, and with him.

Fuck Garth.

And—if the stranger manhandling me through my front door is everything his profile promised—fuck *me*.

I don't even know his name. Nobody who knows me would believe this. But I'm a new man now. I'm done letting my heart get broken.

All I want is a stud to overwhelm me, rail me out of my goddamn mind with his proportionally hung cock, and then leave me the *fuck* alone to keep packing my shit.

Or, you know, eating ice cream and crying... but who's counting?

A wolf-whistle in my ear makes me nearly jump out of

my skin. "Jesus!" I yelp, shoving the guy's chest. "What's that for?"

But I already know. He's staring over my shoulder at the expensive view of Stanley Park and Vancouver's waterfront.

Great. Even tonight, something *can* send my mood crashing through the floor like a ten-ton cannonball en route to the basement laundry room.

"This place all yours?" the guy asks, making my cheeks burn with anger—and humiliation.

He isn't trying to piss me off. But one question and my brain is all too happy to fall into line, singing the silent refrain until my skull echoes with Garth's voice.

This is *his* place, not mine. I'm just an ornament. Indoor topiary. No, worse than that—a garden gnome. Something to be seen and not heard—and eventually, Garth stopped wanting even that much.

My self-respect, my friends, and five years of my life... all gone, just like that. But after everything Garth took from me, I'm taking one thing of my own: a tiny pinch of his galaxy-sized overconfidence.

"What does it matter?" I challenge Mr. Not-So-Right Now.

I've got all the power tonight. I can kick Brad out whenever I want. I don't have to wait for him to tell me he's taking a long break from all my shit, and he expects me to be gone when he gets back in two weeks.

Fuckhead.

And where's Garth now? Some tropical beach, drunk-posting hot pieces of ass while he "recovers" from the "betrayal" of me growing a backbone...

The guy smirks at me. "Thought so," he tells me, casual as anything. "So, which is it? Rich daddy or sugar daddy?"

I think I'm seeing red. "Excuse me?" I ask, ice dripping from every syllable.

The guy pulls away. "Jeez, man. Don't be so touchy. You'll kill the mood."

And I almost fall for it.

A knife tip of loneliness twists between my ribs, and my hard-on pushes insistently against my jeans. But I see the ugly, gleeful look in his eye. He's waiting for me to apologize and beg him to stay.

It's *so* hard not to be tempted.

I need to be touched. Held, picked up, crushed against Brad's body. Thrown onto the bed. Covered with his weight. Fucked, fast and merciless, until my cries echo against every single goddamn floor-to-ceiling window.

But underneath all my desires lies the hard truth: I've never been able to resist a guy who doesn't even want me half as badly as I want him.

It started with Carter Haywood, and it never really stopped.

Shit.

Maybe I'll never get what I really want, but I'm done settling for second-best.

"You should go," I tell him.

"What the fuck?" Just like Garth, the moment he doesn't get what he wants without reservation, the mask falls away. He sneers at me. "Man, you're a real piece of work, you know? Lead a guy on—"

He launches into his rant as I pull back and lead him down the hallway, but I just tune it out. The moment he steps outside and turns to keep belittling me, I let go of the door.

It swings shut in his face, and I turn to head for the bedroom.

It's a miracle: my boner hasn't wilted.

Okay, if I'm being honest with myself, it's not a miracle—it's as predictable as clockwork. Just the thought of Carter's name is enough.

I collapse on the bed and wrestle my clothes off.

After that first year, Garth never bothered finishing me off, so I know the drill. Close my eyes, tug my dick like I'm competing in an all-stars championship, and call up the same fantasies as always.

Me, bent over the locker room bench, clutching on for dear life.

Carter behind, above, inside *me. One fist in my hair and the other hand on my hip.*

Our bodies slamming together. His cock buried balls-deep inside me. His grunts mingling with my whimpers. Louder, faster, harder, more more more—

My phone just lit up.

And I *know* I didn't give that random guy my number… but I can't help glancing at my screen.

Garth.

Of course it is.

"Fuck," I groan at the phone. My dick throbs in protest against my fingers. "Fuck you *so* much."

I've checked the place a dozen times over for hidden cameras. It's just bad luck. But with his presence suddenly looming large over me again, I can't bring myself to keep going.

Okay. I'll just read it and keep going.

I'll be back tomorrow night. Work needs me.

Shit. I should have expected that.

Keeping one hand on my semi, more out of hope than expectation, I peck out my response with one thumb.

I'm not done packing.

His answer comes within seconds.

You have until 5pm. My people will finish up. Send me your forwarding address.

Holy shit.

I don't even want to figure out a response to that. So I let my phone thump against my chest and squeeze myself gently, letting spite fuel me. I need a few minutes to forget everyone but me.

Even Carter.

There. It's happening again. It always works, no matter what.

Heat makes my belly tense up, and then a fresh wave of sparks tingles along my skin, electric and sharp.

Fuck it.

I grab my phone, blindly swipe away from the messages, and open up YouTube. When the autocomplete history pops up, I scan it.

Carter Haywood locker room interview wardrobe malfunction
Carter Haywood hockey team charity car wash
Carter Haywood summer workout routine
Carter Haywood underwear photo shoot

Yeah. I'm gonna treat myself to that last one. I tap it, and before the ads are over I'm stroking myself again. I want to be ready when my favorite photo comes up in three and a half minutes.

Blackness closes around my field of vision, and I lose myself in the bliss as I writhe in the sweat-soaked sheets until the final surge of heat slams into me.

Why the hell did I bother with Grindr? Hell, with Garth? This is all I need. Or, at the very least, it's time to accept the truth.

This is all I'm ever going to get.

CHAPTER

One

FELIX

"Catch."

"*Augh!*"

The noise I make is like a dying whoopee cushion. I stumble on the slippery concrete ramp, nearly flinging my phone straight up in the air as I bring my hands up to protect my face.

Who in their right mind would throw me anything? It's been a few years since high school gym class, but I can sense incoming expected masculinity a mile off. Doesn't mean I'm going to be able to catch whatever it is.

Splash.

Shit. That's the sound of a rope hitting water.

To be precise, a bowline from the tiny barge that's currently bringing me half of my worldly possessions.

Now that my pretty nose is safe, I peek through my fingers to assess the situation.

It's... not great.

My first problem is the bowline bobbing in the waves. It's

five feet away already, and drifting further—along with the boat it's supposed to be mooring.

My second problem is Captain Murphy. The skipper of Sunrise Island's one and only barge isn't a cheerful guy at the best of times. Even while we were growing up, I'm not sure I ever saw him smile.

And Murph's about to learn to walk on water, just so he can throttle me.

The third problem? Never in a million years would I have imagined *this*.

"Is... is... a-are those—" I stutter.

"Shoe boxes?" Murph cuts the engine. "If it walks like a shoebox, quacks like a shoebox..." He shuffles along the side of the boat, heaves a terse sigh, and starts hauling in the rope. "I left my guy with the other half of your stuff. But if we don't hurry, I can't make it to the next job."

Shoeboxes.

Garth Motherfucking Roberts hired people to pack the rest of my stuff into *shoeboxes*.

"Other half of my..." I trail off, still staring at the barge.

Murph doesn't say any more than that, but the guilt still hits me like a ten-ton brick. He's already doing me a big favour by squeezing in one trip with less than a day's notice.

I've been wrong about one thing: Garth *did* listen to me sometimes.

He knew exactly how to plan the worst possible day of my life.

"Ready?"

Salt water drips from the loop of rope in Murph's hand.

It would really help if I could stop imagining how heavy it is, and what will happen to me when I inevitably get concussed, swept out to sea. I bet I'll get found three weeks later by the Coast Guard. Naked and clinging to a hunk of driftwood. Living off seaweed and whatever fish I can catch with my bare hands...

"Felix!"

"R-Ready!" I spread both hands, imagining myself as a goalie defending a net, but I probably look more like that scene from Titanic.

Murph flings the rope.

I lurch forward.

All the consequences arrive at once.

I flailed for the rope, my feet slipped across the algae, the world lurched toward me, the rope magically appeared in my hands, and...

And now I'm in the ocean.

"Shit shit shit shit ow argh shit fuck—" I yelp, scrambling to my feet and back up the ramp.

Cold cold ouch wet oh fuck cold ouch my palms and is that my knee and ow fuck cold...!

I'm soaking wet and numb from the waist down.

At least my instincts worked: hang onto the rope, and get away from the water. The barge is close enough that Murph hops off it. He's prising the rope off my hands and mooring the barge.

"Fuck!" I whimper, jamming my fingertips into my soaking wet pockets to find my phone.

Dead. Of course. Turns out my day *can* get worse.

"You all right?" Murph grunts. There's no slippery death trap algae beyond the high tide line, but he ushers me away from the boat and up to the gravel road anyway. It's clear he's not going to let me help unload.

"Uh, yeah. Yeah. Um. I'm fine," I shake my head. It's a warm spring day, so I'm not going to die of frostbite, just mortification. That feels way more pressing right now. I have to say something. "Murph. God, I'm sorry. I had no idea—"

Murph claps my shoulder and squeezes once. "Guy's a douchebag." Then he strides back down the ramp to the barge.

I'm floored. I've never seen Murph be that nice to *anyone*. I'm not used to seeing anyone be nice to anyone lately.

But this is why I'm coming home.

My chest goes tight, and I press my hand against it as I blink back the tears.

Murph must have taped together the shoeboxes into big, cube-shaped bundles. One at a time, he's hauling them to the top of the ramp. And I'm the kind of twink who gets a sprain grinding coffee, but I feel bad just standing here.

"What can I do?"

"Frog? If he's running today."

"Ohhh. Yeah," I smack myself in the forehead, turning to look around.

There's only one car on Sunrise Island: Ladybird, our universally-beloved ceremonial red vintage Beetle. If I asked to borrow her to move house, I'd never live down the scandal.

The only vehicles allowed are golf carts. If someone sells theirs, everyone scrambles up the hierarchy like hermit crabs exchanging shells. I'm a brand new crab without a shell… so I get to borrow the loaner golf cart, AKA Frog.

Sunrise's most notorious villain is hideous, lime-green, and doesn't go faster than five miles an hour. And, like Murph just reminded me, that's on the days he runs at all.

And I don't see him anywhere.

Worst.

Day.

Ever.

I shield my eyes, pointlessly scanning the gravel road again. All I see are a couple of wheelbarrows—the truly entry-level vehicle—and some kids' bikes.

What am I going to do? Lash a wheelbarrow to a bike? Pedal home with teetering stacks of shoeboxes, my knees by my ears?

May as well put on a big red nose and sell popcorn, like a fucking clown.

The thump behind me announces that Murph just set down the last of the shoebox piles. "I'm heading back for the rest," he tells me. "I'll be about an hour. If you're not here, should I leave it here?"

I pinch the bridge of my nose and nod. As nice as he's being, Murph will run straight into the Pacific Ocean if I start crying in front of him. "Thanks, man."

Murph grunts again as he retreats to the boat.

I hold it together until the engine kicks on and sputters into the distance. And then I let the tears roll down my face as I march down the gravel road.

Frog was supposed to be here, waiting for me, and obviously he's not. But in the row of a dozen parked wheelbarrows, there *is* one that catches my eye... the kind that's a fancy four-wheeled yard cart.

I'm going to steal a wheelbarrow.

Temporarily, of course. I'll bake an apology pie. But this still isn't how I wanted to start my first full day back on Sunrise Island.

Mind made up, I haul the cart toward the boat ramp, and then I start wrestling the first cube of shoeboxes on top of it. Physical labour isn't my thing, but everything is ten times worse when my palms are still raw and stinging from my boat ramp fall.

"Fuck Garth," I grunt. "And fuck me. And fuck me for fucking him. And fuck him for—"

I'm too sweaty and out of breath to swear *and* wrestle.

Once the damn thing is finally balanced, I cross myself and pray that my unsafe load stays intact. Otherwise I'm gonna end up leaving a trail of dandruff shampoo and embarrassing teenage diaries.

I can't believe Garth won again.

As always, I'm the butt of the joke.

Every squelching step feels more and more like I'm pushing my temporarily-stolen wheelbarrow right back into the past I've been trying so desperately to leave behind.

Wait. Is that…?

"Frog!"

I'm at the top of Holy Fudge Hill, and the useless hunk of metal I've been cussing out is at the bottom.

I cover my mouth with one hand, clutching my chest with the other. I can barely contain all the hope suddenly filling me past bursting. If I can get Frog back up and running… maybe, just maybe, today will finally get better.

Vrrrr—

"Oh, *shit!*"

It's a rookie mistake. I'm used to wheelbarrows staying where you put them, so I let go of the cart handle. And this street is nicknamed Holy Fudge Hill for a reason.

"No no no no stop ohmygodpleasestop shiiiit—!"

However hard I sprint, I can't catch up. It's picking up speed too fast, still headed straight downhill.

Toward Frog, and whoever's crouched over the golf cart engine.

Oh. My. God.

My panic is suddenly a full-blown freakout. Stealing a wheelbarrow is nothing compared to killing one of my new neighbours.

"Look out!" I holler.

The tape gives way around the shoebox cube. Everything is flying off the cart, across the gravel road and into the ditch on one side, thorny blackberry bushes on the other.

Now I'm going so fast I can't stop, either. My arms windmill frantically as I dodge lids and boxes, clothes and books, and *definitely at least one dildo oh my god just kill me now please—*

Then the guy shields his eyes and looks up.

My heart slams against my rib cage. My stomach drops through my feet. I can hardly remember my own name. I'm running faster than my feet can keep up, and my world is standing still.

Holy fucking crap.

It's Carter Haywood.

CHAPTER Two

CARTER

I NEVER EXPECTED TO COME HOME SO SOON.

Not that I've had a lot of time to think about it. Even before I left for boarding school ten years ago, I lived, breathed, sweated, bled, and dreamed hockey.

Then I blinked and found myself at the peak of my career. Press clamouring around me, crowds cheering my name, autographing jerseys after every game... And the rest of it, too. I love the rest of it just as much. Identical protein-packed meals, gym routines, sports massages, even the endless drills.

I gave up everything for the game, and I never wanted it any other way.

Until a month ago.

That's when I went from flying on ice to falling hard and fast, right from the peak of my career. All it took was one collision. Then a whole new whirlwind began: a hospital trip, two hip surgeries, and a spot on the injured reserve list.

Maybe permanently.

Dammit! I'm thinking about it again.

I can't help it, though.

The very next game after my injury, my team got knocked out of the running for the Cup. It feels like my fault, and I know the headlines agreed.

They've forgotten all that now. Everyone just wants to know what happens next: my agent, my team manager, and what feels like countless tens of thousands of fans.

Will Canada's prodigy-turned-superstar ever take the ice again?

All I can say is the same line, over and over: *If I can, I will.*

I wish I could say I'm more interested in questions about my future mobility than my ice time, but we all know where my priorities lie. I wouldn't have got this far without being obsessed with the game.

"Come on," I grunt into Frog's engine. "Work with me."

But when I lean around to turn the key, he just sputters, coughs once, and goes silent again.

I groan and smack the dashboard, but my second and third attempts end just the same.

"Fine," I grunt, tossing my wrench down into my metal toolbox. "Stay here on the side of the road. See if I care."

I miss, and the wrench lands with a sharp thud on the gravel.

"Motherfucker!" I flip it off.

I'm not on the good painkillers anymore, so the wrench doesn't rise to the bait. Instead, I can nearly hear Coach Dawson's voice in my head.

Cool it, Cart. Save it for the face-off.

Shit. This isn't me.

But I guess I'm used to pouring out all my worries and frustrations on the ice. After a month off, my veins feel full of fire. I'm a simmering volcano waiting to blow... and I don't have any release outlets.

I take a couple of deep breaths, resting the side of my head on the roll bar of the golf cart.

It was nice of Berty Baker, long-time president of Sunrise Island Residents, to loan me Frog. It's nobody's fault the stupid thing has died three times in two days.

Even as desperate for distraction as I am, I'd rather limp half a mile to the ferry and back than go over every part of this engine one more time.

There must be a ghost. It's the only explanation.

"Okay. Let's go," I grumble, gripping the side of the golf cart and lowering myself onto my good knee. Then I scoop up the wrench and set it gently in the toolbox.

Frog sways alarmingly when I try to pull on the side to get back up again, so I hastily let go.

"Shit."

At least none of my neighbours are witnessing this.

Carter Haywood, former all-star, stuck on his knees on a rural gravel road.

No, I'm not stuck. I *can* get up by myself. It just takes a while. And looks pretty weird for people who remember the energetic kid I used to be.

The embarrassment still tastes bitter.

"I'm buying a new golf cart tomorrow," I growl at Frog. "I don't care if I have to buy my own barge to get it here."

Gravel crunches nearby.

Well, fuck. I'm not alone anymore.

Someone's coming along to gently console me about my career and tell me to pop by if I need milk or sugar or anything.

Wait—is that a shriek?

Someone needs help.

Instinct kicks in. I grab the golf cart and push myself up to my feet as fast as I can, straightening up and shielding my eyes.

And then I see it: a metal cart careening down Holy Fudge Hill, stuff flying every which way from it like Santa's sleigh.

Wait. Are those *shoeboxes* bouncing across the road and bursting open? They must be, but I don't see any shoes.

None of this makes sense. I'm definitely not on the good painkillers anymore, right? No way—my hip aches pretty bad from that sudden leap to my feet.

Someone's running downhill after the cart, futilely chasing it. His arms are flailing wildly as he leaps like Santa's least graceful reindeer across the flying debris.

I can only think of one person who makes that noise— and who would end up in this exact situation.

Little Fox Harris?

"Look out!"

No way. It's him.

Fox stumbles to a halt, and my heart leaps into my throat.

He's right. His wagon is heading straight toward Frog… and it's going fast enough that it might just tip over the rickety old three-wheeled golf cart.

Right onto me.

I stumble backward, just praying I can move fast enough to escape the collision.

Crash!

My heart pounds at the sound of metal on metal. I'm just barely clear of the golf cart, but that's enough.

A shoebox hits me in the knees, and then another one. The impact sent them flying every which way as the wagon crumples into Frog's side. Then the golf cart rises up off the ground and sways.

I hold my breath and wait.

But Frog slowly sinks to all three wheels again, shoving the wagon backward as gravity wins.

Speaking of...

I can hardly believe who's stumbling to a halt in front of me.

"It's you," I manage, from the distant part of my brain that isn't a dumbstruck statue.

Felix Harris, my best friend's little brother.

I always thought of it as Alph's house, not Felix's. But I spent just about every waking minute there, outside of school or practice. Alph's little brother was always skulking around and watching us, so we started calling him Fox.

This is so weird.

Not just the fact that I see echoes of the kid I remember from all those years ago in the face of the man he's become.

But why the hell does my world feel like it's narrowed to a single point?

If this were old times, I'd be laughing and making fun of all the carnage he's caused. But suddenly, I can barely even make out our surroundings.

All I can do is gawk at him and the ways he's changed.

He's... grown up. I mean, *duh*. I'm the same age as Alph, and he's three years younger. So he's, what, twenty-three?

He's always been built a little more delicate than his brother and me. But his shoulders have filled out, and the sweat-soaked T-shirt clings to his chest in a whole new way.

Fox is still a few inches shorter than me, and his eyes are still that bright green that always caught me off-guard.

That stare used to unsettle me—frustrating me in his

bratty moments, and clinging to me when Alph and I closed the bedroom door to keep him out.

Now his gaze does something else completely.

Holy shit. My jeans feel tight all of a sudden.

It's the adrenaline. It's gotta be. There's no other reason.

I've been around plenty of sweaty men in stinky locker rooms. I would have noticed if the solution to my chronic single status was... well, men.

But one look at Fox's lithe body under his shirt, and I'm suddenly noticing the print of his bulge between his legs with way too much interest.

What the hell?

I don't know what's happening, but this isn't some "passing breeze, easy boner" situation.

Wait. Wait a goddamn minute, Cart. Think with your upstairs brain.

"Jesus! Fox? Are you okay?"

I step toward him as my old instinct rises—protective, yet equally amused and irritated at all the trouble that follows him around.

That much is familiar. The force of it takes me aback, and so do the newer parts of it.

The way I want to wrap my arms around him and warm him up with my body, wrestle off his wet clothes, shove him down on his back as he stares up at me with those not-so-innocent green eyes...

Whoa.

"Fox?" I prompt when he doesn't say anything for a few moments. He's still just staring at me.

"Carter?" Fox finally whispers, and I think I understand what falling in love feels like.

Shiiiiit.

CHAPTER Three

CARTER

This can't be happening.

It's just a passing thing. An impulse. I need an outlet for all my frustrations.

Despite all attempts to convince myself otherwise, Fox's voice ripples down my spine and flows into my veins like honey.

I swallow hard, searching for something to say. I need to stop staring at Felix's mouth, and the pretty red colour of his lower lip… right the hell now.

Come on. Joke around. Be normal.

"Yeah, it's me," I grunt. "You look like you swam here. Did you?"

It would be just like the Fox I once knew to follow some hare-brained idea about kayaking here, even though he's a walking disaster. That wouldn't explain the boxes, though.

"No." Fox doesn't laugh. Instead, his hands rise toward his chest, a familiar little gesture like he's trying to pull himself together.

I feel way worse than I expected about trying to make fun

of him. My throat is tight with guilt, and my chest aches. I... I kind of want to hug him? And apologize? What the hell?

I can't believe I enjoyed teasing little Fox all those years ago. Suddenly, I'd lift an overturned golf cart just to stop anything from hurting him—even accidentally.

Whoa. His palms.

"Fox! You're bleeding?" I step forward and I barely stop myself from grabbing for his hands to inspect them.

He's a grown man. I'm sure he knows.

"Uh..." Felix blinks. "You called me Fox."

Okay. Maybe he doesn't know. He's more spacey than usual, and I'm starting to get seriously worried that he's in shock.

I have to look after him. He's coming inside, and I'll make him lie down and give him something sweet.

Absolutely not my cock... no matter how weirdly interested it is.

I try my hardest not to think about the twitch in my pants at the idea. My breathing is a little heavier all of a sudden, too.

"You've always been Fox," I tell him with a shrug. "Right?"

"Nobody else has—I mean..." He rubs his temples. "Why are you here?"

I squint at him. "I didn't think I got voted off the island."

Pink rises to his cheeks—and how weird is it that I'm suddenly fixated on how adorable he looks when he blushes? "I mean, uh... sorry," he stutters. "Your team. Are you guys out...?"

Oh. Of course he hasn't seen the headlines. He was never into sports like me and Alph. As far as he knows, I'm supposed to be playing a quarter-final or something for the Cup.

"We're out," I grunt. Then I clear my throat and run my

hand across the close-cropped hair at the back of my head. "And I'm out, for now."

His eyes widen. "What? *Out* out?" He stares at me like he can't believe it.

"Yeah, *out* out," I echo him, and I brace myself for the pity that always comes at this moment.

Fox's jaw drops. "That's... huge," he whispers. And then he has the weirdest reaction. He starts to smile, like he still can't believe his ears but he's about to congratulate me.

Wait. Shit.

Fox has been openly gay for longer than I can remember. Of course he's not talking about the game.

"The game, I mean!" I blurt out hastily. Heat flushes up the back of my neck to the tips of my ears, and I'm pretty sure I'm turning the colour of a tomato. "Out of the game. Not, you know..."

"*Oh!*" Fox's voice almost squeaks, and then we stare at each other like neither of us know what to say.

I'm not sure which of us laughs first, but thank God one of us does. It breaks the ice—so to speak—and suddenly we're both laughing together in a way that feels altogether new.

Like friends.

Thank God the tension is broken. "You need to get warm and dry," I tell him. "The rest of it can wait."

"But I... all my stuff..." Fox trails off, staring forlornly at the mess. His shoulders sink, and he looks like he's crumpling in on himself. "I'll be in the others' way."

Fuck.

I've seen him quiet. I've seen him annoyed. I've even seen him look at me reproachfully for hiding away with Alph and not letting him into our treehouse.

But I've never seen him like this before. He's haunted by some shadow I have no way of knowing, but I can see the edges of it: he's afraid to take up space.

As much as he skulked around spying on his big brother, trying to make himself a part of our friendship... he wasn't *afraid*. Just aloof. The look on his face now is all wrong.

"Hey, listen. That's my new place," I point out the porch just visible around the blackberry bushes. "It's not locked. Grab a warm shower. I've got lots of spare clothes."

"Are you sure?" Fox murmurs, still staring at all his things. Not even a wisecrack about me having learned to bake. He really *is* out of it.

"I'm sure," I tell him.

Without thinking, I reach out to squeeze his shoulder for a moment. And it's like touching bottled lightning. A pulse of it shivers through my body, making every hair on my forearms stand on end.

The trail burns right the way down the middle of my body, all the way to the core of my belly.

My still-hard dick isn't getting any softer with the way he's staring at me, all wide green eyes and soft-looking parted lips.

Oh, shit. Shit, that wasn't supposed to happen!

I'm still holding onto him. I just grin like it's old times, let go of his shoulder, and make as if I'm going to shove him toward the house. "Go on."

"Fine, fine," he grumbles, raising his hands and giving in to my nagging. But I can't bring myself to smile, because he turns and trudges toward my house, shoulders slumped and one hand on his forehead.

Fuck.

The poor guy. It's obvious he feels horrible about... well, everything. And I want to help.

It takes everything I've got to stop myself from following Fox inside. Instead, I wait until he's out of sight and then prise apart the wagon and golf cart.

After I've straightened out the wagon wheels, I start crouching awkwardly to grab shoeboxes. One at a time, I shove them back inside and close them up, adding them to the precarious stack.

Obviously I can't help noticing the contents of some of them, but I'm trying my hardest to be a gentleman about it.

One last scan of the ditch and bushes for crop tops, magazines... and, ahem, suction cup dildos... and I'm done.

That took longer than I thought, and my hip aches a lot worse now. I tug the wagon along at a slow limping pace. Once I make it to my driveway, I leave it there and turn toward the house.

A trail of wet footprints leads around to the side door. And just the sight makes my heart do that weird little leaping thing again.

Fuck.

Something's different.

Those butterflies are back in my stomach. I haven't felt so nervous since my first face-off in my junior season. And there isn't even a good reason. Just Fox's presence.

It's not because of the accident, is it?

A month ago, I could stare anyone down without fear. Even bullies on skates—which Fox has never been, on either count.

But it isn't fear that's gripping me. It only feels like it because whatever it is, it's equally unfamiliar.

Do I even want to admit to myself that I know what it is?

No. I must be wrong.

I press my hand on my chest for a moment like Fox does, but it doesn't calm me down. So instead, I grip the doorknob and lean into this feeling.

It's like a tide is pulling me towards something new, yet inevitable. And, most dangerous of all, *thrilling*. And I'm not going to be able to fight it for long.

For the first time in my life... I want to yield.

CHAPTER *Four*

FELIX

This is a nightmare.

I made an absolute idiot of myself in front of Carter fucking Haywood.

And I can't help noticing that I'm still kinda into him.

Okay, fine. I can't lie to myself. There's no "kind of" about it—I'm excruciatingly into him.

The moment I saw him at the bottom of Holy Fudge Hill, it was like no time at all had passed. I was right back to that old, familiar feeling—I just wanted so badly for him to *see* me.

God. I really should have been more specific.

I actually want him to see me as *cool*. Instead, he saw a walking disaster ruining Sunrise's only loaner golf cart, *and* a stranger's stolen wagon, while covering the road in all my worldly possessions.

Guilt and yearning are sharp in my stomach, familiar twin aches. But they can never hold a candle to the desire that burns through me.

Fuck, I want him. One touch of his strong hand on my

shoulder, one sniff of that rough, masculine scent of him that I thought I'd never smell again…

I'm *aching* for it, and it hurts twice as bad to know I'm just making it all up in my head.

Again.

"Fuck," I grimace, wiping my face with the side of my hand, then my hand on the only dry part of my T-shirt. I don't know how long I've been sitting here on the shoe bench of Carter's hallway, stewing in self-pity.

I really did intend to go upstairs and shower. But I chose the side entrance to avoid dripping seawater everywhere, and as soon as I let myself in, I found a row of neatly-packed, perfectly normal sized cardboard boxes all the way down the hall.

It shouldn't have been a surprise. He's obviously just moved back, or I would have heard about it before now. And normal cardboard boxes are how normal people move house.

Just not in my life, which is so far past absurd that I can't even laugh at it anymore.

I still can't do anything right, and Carter still can't do anything wrong.

Who the hell am I, imagining that his looks contain a fraction of the longing and desire that I feel—that I've tried for years to forget?

He's been nice to me so far. But it won't be long before he's back to irritated glances and dismissive jokes.

Sure, I made all those resolutions not to fall into the same trap as before. But I've always had an exception—and it's the origin of all the rest.

Carter Haywood is my weak spot. Always has been, always will be.

I'm going to lap up whatever he gives me, so long as it means he's noticing me.

My first warning that I'm about to be interrupted is Carter flicking on the light switch on me in all my miserable glory.

I launch myself to my feet, which at least is better than being glued to the shoe bench by my own self-pity.

"What the—" he stares at me, obviously perplexed.

"I'm sorry I didn't hear you and I got distracted—" *Stop talking, Felix. Just stop while you're ahead.* "But I'm not being weird!"

Okay. Great. Kill me now.

At least I manage to shut my mouth now, before I apologize for something weirdly specific like making him think I'm stealing his underwear.

Which I definitely wouldn't have until I thought about it, but now that I have, it sounds like a way better idea than it actually would be.

Carter's whole forehead crinkles and lifts up a little, like he can't figure out what to make of me.

Shit. There's that look again—the one I hoped I'd never see again.

There's my best friend's weird little kid brother.

"Sorry," I mumble again, flinching toward the door to escape while I'm... not ahead, but at least I haven't dug myself the deepest pit known to mankind.

"Whoa, whoa," Carter soothes me, raising both hands like I'm a startled horse. "Sit down again. My bad. I shouldn't have startled you."

"No, I—I was supposed to be..." I turn, looking for a staircase. I don't see one, so I point at a random door and hope for the best. "Going upstairs?"

Carter's eyes crinkle with amusement. And I'm not sure if I'm fooling myself into thinking that his expression isn't dismissive anymore, but... tentative. Gentle, even.

"That's the laundry room. But yeah, I thought you were showering, not turning into a Foxsicle. What's up?"

God almighty, I wish he wouldn't call me that.

My thighs quiver. My toes curl into my soaking wet sneakers, and soaking wet denim stretches tight across my semi.

It's not because I don't like the nickname. It's just the opposite.

I forgot the way he says it. The way his syllables round themselves out, the X slides from his tongue in a familiar hiss, and I'm pretty sure he makes the nickname longer than my real name is.

Maybe that's just because it always feels like the world is standing still when he says my name.

"I, um..." I stutter, dropping my gaze as I sink down onto the bench again, my hands covering my face.

Don't look at him.

I'll only blush and lose track of my tongue and say something stupid, like, *How long was I sitting here fantasizing about you?*

"Got lost in your thoughts?"

Whoa. I'm so attuned to his presence that I feel the heat of him moving past me. His smell—the intoxicating rush of it—follows, and sound is only my third clue as to Carter's whereabouts.

As I open my eyes again, I swallow hard. He's crouching—no, he's kneeling in front of me, but slowly and with a groan. Like he's aching from moving house—or fixing the engine.

Of course. He's been trying to fix Frog for me. And I just fucked him up instead.

I groan softly. "I'm sorry," I mumble, barely able to look at him.

I feel small again, all of a sudden. Like he and Alph are looking at my skinned knee and telling me I'll be fine, that it'll make me get tough. I distinctly remember crying while running to ask Mom how to exfoliate my knees.

"For what?" Carter asks, his voice light. "Shit happens."

"To me, yeah."

"Especially to you," Carter agrees. "Now, we're going to get those shoes off," he tells me. "And then you shower. You're gonna get hypothermia like that."

I flinch, hard.

Ouch.

I knew it. Or I should have known.

He's doing it again: treating me like the kid brother. So long as that's who I am to him, I'll always be at arm's length. Or shut out on the other side of the door.

I'm not going to cry about it, though. The old me would have. But I'm *not* the old me anymore, even if all my yearning makes me feel like no time at all has passed.

The new me has learned his lesson. I can't get my heart involved again. And I'm not going to keep fooling myself about men. Especially this one. I'll lust after Carter, but that's all.

He's not getting the power to break my heart again—without ever even knowing it.

When I open my eyes, Carter's still on his knees, but he's rummaging through a box nearby. "I oughta have some spare shoes."

I snort. "Not in my size. It's fine. I have more at home."

"You're not putting these back on," Carter pokes at my shoe, and I blush at the puddles of salt water I've already left on the hardwood floor.

"I'll go barefoot."

Carter's brows shoot up almost into his hairline. He doesn't even have to say a word. He just gives me an incredulous look. Any kid who's grown up here knows that you don't walk barefoot on the gravel roads.

I know I've lost this argument, but the real point is way more important.

"Carter," I tell him, swallowing back the instinctive rush of butterflies that awakens in me at the sound of his name. "I'm not Alph's little brother anymore, you know."

Carter blinks, and then he braces himself with a hand on the bench next to me. "I know," he says quietly.

Yet he's still here kneeling in front of me, like I'm a wounded little bird that he's trying his best to fix up.

Is he laughing at me? I don't think so. I can't find even a trace of a joke in his eyes.

Carter is serious.

And the longer the silence stretches out, the more I feel that strange *charge* between us. I'm more and more sure that I'm not making up this unsettled new feeling between us.

The air is crackling with it. "Okay," I whisper. "Good."

Carter nods once, without the usual calm conviction that underscores his every action. This time, it's slow and tentative. And he's studying my face like it's his only map to somewhere—and I have no idea what that's about.

Then he leans over and puts one big hand on my shoulder again, gives a comforting squeeze.

I think it's supposed to be comforting, anyway. It's never going to calm me down, feeling that touch and the forbidden rush of fantasies that pour into me. My body is suddenly *wired* like he's connected the last circuit and energy is rushing through my veins.

My heart pounds like crazy. My lips feel dry, and even licking them doesn't seem to help. All I can think about is how badly I want his hand to slide down my shoulder, to take my hand.

Or my thigh. Or my dick...

Holy fuck.

His hand *is* on my thigh. What's happening?

My eyes snap open as I stare down at him—on his knees, on the floor, his hands on *my* knees as he looks up at me.

"Shoes," is all he says, which ought to dispel all my fantasies.

Instead, it gives them life.

Carter has always been this huge, strong, silent entity—never giving in and giving me what I want, always unknowable and distant. But here he is, on his knees in front of me, his whole attention upon me.

Whether or not he's got his hands in my pants is basically irrelevant to this fantasy.

I gulp and nod. I'm afraid to blink and miss a second. And I definitely can't say a word. Something else might escape—like a whimper, or a moan, or a plea: *touch me, please, anywhere you want, any way you want...*

My cold fingers lost the battle with the soaked knots of my shoelaces. But despite how big Carter's hands are, his touch is nimble. He delicately teases apart the mess I made until the knots are loose, and then slips them free.

Oh, fuck.

There must be some way I can invent to make his palm brush against my throbbing cock, even slightly and accidentally. My heart is thudding so fast in my ears that I can barely think over the noise.

"I—I can't do this," I whisper. I can't help the ragged, desperate desire in my voice. All I can do is hope he mistakes it for something else. "I gotta go."

Carter looks up at me and stubbornly takes hold of one foot at a time, easing off my shoes. "Not in these."

It isn't a suggestion, either. It's an order—and that fills my brain with hot, crackling static that washes away all other thoughts.

I want him.

And he's going to figure it out.

Things are in motion that I can't stop now. All Carter has to do is notice… well, literally anything. And he might be oblivious, but he's not stupid.

And then what happens?

Once my shoes are off, Carter braces himself on the bench again. This time, his hand is a lot closer to the outside of my thigh than before. And he stays there, on his knees.

Wait. Wait a *goddamn* minute. Maybe I'm the oblivious one here…

No. I can't let myself have that much hope. My fantasy is about to come crashing down like it always does.

The facts are just… the facts.

Carter's pupils are huge, and he's breathing fast.

He's staying where he is, between my knees, for way longer than any old straight friend would.

And he's looking slowly up at me, inspecting every inch of me in a way I don't think I've ever been looked at before.

When he gets to my crotch—the clearly visible swell against my jeans—his gaze stops and lingers there.

My cheeks flush with heat. I try to put together an apology, parting my lips to catch my breath. But I can't stop the way my dick swells under his gaze, pushing insistently at my jeans.

"I have to get my boxes," I whisper raggedly.

Carter tilts his head like he's confused. "Oh. Yeah. I already did."

I blink sluggishly at him, struggling to register anything that isn't the heat of his body so close to mine. Only a level of kindness I've hardly experienced could break through this dizzying fog.

"You... did?" I whisper, and my traitorous heart does its best to ignore my new rule.

"It was nothing," Carter grunts.

"I-I mean, I have more boxes coming. I have to get those, too."

"Then we better get moving." Carter winces as he slowly pushes himself to his feet.

Suddenly I'm aware of it: he's not moving quite right.

"Shit. Are you okay?" I whisper, biting my lip.

He grimaces and looks away from me, then rolls his shoulders back when he's upright again and nods. "I'll be fine. I'll help you move."

"That's okay, I'll—" I start, but he interrupts.

"That isn't an offer. Now, come on. Shower's upstairs."

His retreating back holds none of the answers to the questions that are racing through my brain. So I peel off my socks, hopping from one foot to the other, and then I pad barefoot after him.

This can't be happening.

But the facts are piling up, and every time I take a breath I feel like I'm getting higher off the fantasy I want to make out of them.

Is this really happening?

There's only one way to find out.

CHAPTER
Five

CARTER

I hope it sounds like I have a plan, because the truth is... I really don't.

Who knows what's about to happen between us? Maybe this—whatever *this* is—will be strictly platonic.

Yeah, yeah, and maybe pigs fly.

I built my playboy reputation carefully, but it's all unsubstantiated rumour. I never let myself focus on anyone—or anything, really—besides the game. I didn't want to risk losing the future I wanted more than anything.

Now I might be losing that future anyway, and this is moving way faster than I imagined... and I can't stop flirting with disaster. And of course it couldn't just be *any* disaster... it had to be Fox Harris.

But he won't stop penetrating my very soul with that precious, green gaze that awakens things I never thought I could feel. He makes me want to beat the very world away from his doorstep.

I don't know what life has handed him these past few

years, but Fox is even more lost than I am. He needs someone to remind him that he can save himself.

For some crazy reason, I'm starting to think that's me.

I have to do a better job, then. I shouldn't have left him alone. What if he'd really been in shock?

Guilt simmers in the pit of my stomach. I should have made sure he got inside and safely into the shower before going back out to gather up the boxes. But I didn't want to slow him down.

And, to be honest, there's something else.

I didn't want him to see me like this—struggling to walk down the street. Pretty stupid of me, huh? I can't hide it now.

It's taking me a few seconds to manage each step. We're only at the landing halfway up the stairs, and I'm leaning harder on the handrail than I did at the bottom.

The whole way up, Fox has stayed behind me, and silent as… well, as a mouse. But as I push myself away from the railing to head for the other side and the second half of the stairs, he brushes past me and offers his arm.

There's no getting away. I forgot how good he is at getting right in my way when he wants something. And right now he wants to help.

I don't *need* help. My hip hurts pretty badly now, but I'm not going to trip over my own feet.

"I'm fine—"

"Bullshit," Fox cuts me off before I can even finish my lie. As I stare at him, he lifts his chin to stare me in the eye. "If you want me to let you help me, it has to go both ways. Otherwise I'm just your little brother, aren't I?"

I blink a few times as it sinks in.

Shit. I think he's right.

If I rescue him from his shitty day while hiding anything

that makes *me* feel vulnerable, then I can't really be his friend, can I?

My sigh slips out as I give in. "Fine," I mutter, carefully gripping his forearm before we limp across the landing. "But if I fall over, I'm taking you down too."

"Is that a promise?"

"Wh—" I stumble against the front door mat, but Fox's grip is surprisingly strong as he keeps me upright.

Okay, so I almost did trip over my own feet. But that was *so* not my fault.

I can't stop thinking about what Fox meant. I can't come up with any other meaning besides the obvious one.

He wants me on top of him.

And every fibre of my body wants to be there, too—pressing his lithe body into the floor. I want my hands gliding along his bare skin until he's moaning, yielding to my touch, falling apart.

I barely know what I'm doing, but the enthusiasm, the sheer force of the desire rising inside me feels like it will make up for any shortcomings. I want to press myself against his stubborn pieces until he yields to bliss and falls apart in my hands.

And there's more. So much more I want to do with, for, and to him. Anything he wants to do, everything he's dreamed of. Whatever I can learn from him to make up for lost time.

I can't pretend for a moment this is platonic, can I?

I barely even know how we ended up here. One moment, I was kneeling in front of Fox, trading a certain familiar pain for an unfamiliar, tempting pleasure... and the next, we're here.

"So what happened?" Fox asked as I shift myself to the

handrail. He falls into step behind me again, which is a small mercy.

This way, I don't have to look him in the eye.

"Collision, mid-game. Knocked me off my feet. Hips blew out. Two surgeries later, they found torn muscles and missing cartilage. But I'm walking again pretty fast, so my chances are good."

Do I sound like I believe it? There's a mile of difference between *I can climb the stairs in ten times as long as usual* and *I can skate with the pros again.*

"When?" Fox asks.

I don't know what I was expecting, but his question is all matter-of-fact. There's no sugar-coating it. It actually makes me relax a little bit.

"About a month ago."

"Hm," Fox mutters in response. "You still in a lot of pain?"

I shrug with one shoulder, keeping my eyes fixed on the landing. We're almost there. Just a couple more stairs, and I can turn the conversation to something else...

"So, yes. And it's worse when you kneel, right?" Fox asks.

We've only got two more steps, so I wait until we're at the top.

Shoot. I was kind of hoping he'll forget about it, but he's looking at me expectantly.

"Yeah, it does. But don't worry about it."

Fox arches one eyebrow. "Sure. The way you didn't worry about me being soaking wet and possibly in shock."

Our relationship is obviously changing fast, but it's downright weird to get a lecture from him. And weirder still for him to be right—again.

I clear my throat. "Yeah. Good point. But I don't mind."

"Why?" Fox watches me closely, like it's a test.

Oof.

I'm not used to wanting anything this badly without having any of the right answers. No training, no experience, and definitely no natural aptitude. Just me taking shots in the dark, hoping like hell I'm aiming the right way.

"Does it matter?"

"Yes," Fox says with a thin, dry smile—another glimpse of a whole new side to him, and it's one that shakes me to my core.

Obviously there's things I don't know about him anymore—we haven't seen each other in ten years. The last time our paths crossed, we were just kids. But I know his spirit, and finding it freshly scarred… it hurts me almost as bad as he's been hurt.

"What are you afraid of?" I ask him softly. "That I don't want you around?"

He flinches, and I bite my lip, anxiety rising in my chest.

Is that too far? Have I hurt his feelings?

But then he shakes his head. "That you do."

I stare at him, adding that to the long list of things that confuse me about this newer, older Fox.

"I don't do anything I don't want," I tell him, although I'm pretty sure he knows that about me already. "I might not know what this looks like yet," I gesture clumsily between the two of us, "but I do want you around. And I'm never going to be sorry about it."

Something crumples in his face, and he crosses the distance between us to throw his arms around my neck.

I hug him as tightly as I can, and my whole world seems to dissolve in a shower of sparks I barely know how to contain. Our bodies fit together so perfectly, all the flat planes of his narrow chest fitting perfectly against the curves of my muscular body.

Ohhhhh, *fuck*.

Air rushes to my lungs, and my lips part. My cheeks burn, and I suddenly realize how hard our bodies are pressing together—how obvious my arousal is. But so is his. He's hard and needy against my thigh.

And I want to learn how to satisfy him.

In every single way. All the ways I've felt weird about never wanting before—and now that I do, I wasn't prepared for the intensity of the rush thrumming through my blood.

But if he's afraid of my desire...

"If that's a problem for you—" I hoarsely fumble for words.

Fox just whispers, "Kiss me," and I shiver with a breathless, delighted anticipation.

There are so many reasons I shouldn't... but nothing matters as much as the way his whole body trembles as he says it.

Oh, Fox.

I want to crush him against me in a bear hug until he feels safe, or to hold him as gently as a rare butterfly. Maybe both at once.

I can barely believe the mix of feelings crashing through me as I hold not-so-little Fox Harris by the hips, pulling him into me until it feels like the magnets within us will never pull apart again.

Then he adds, in the softest whisper, "Please?"

With that voice, he could make me do anything in this goddamn world... but I have the strangest feeling that this is all he'll ever ask for.

His desire is beautiful.

Fuck it. There's one more thought that's been looping through my brain since the moment I looked up to see that wagon careening down the hill.

He's beautiful.

My hands instinctively rise to Fox's cheeks. I bend my head as he stretches onto his toes. Our lips meet, and I've only got room for two thoughts in my brain.

First—I thought I'd never get closer to heaven than I've already been. Well, holy shit, I was wrong.

And second—I thought I'd never want anything as bad as I wanted this hockey life. But I was wrong again.

I want Fox even more.

CHAPTER *Six*

FELIX

THIS KISS IS EVERYTHING I'VE EVER DREAMED OF—AND MORE.

I don't even begrudge the twinges of pain in my scraped palms when I press my hands flat on his back. It reminds me that this isn't a perfect yet fleeting fantasy.

I've imagined Carter kissing me a thousand different ways: sweet and soft in the lonely small hours when I doubted anyone would ever look at me the way I see in movies; hard and ferocious when I craved nothing more than the force of a man's desire slamming into me.

But nothing could compare to the truth.

It's like sunshine floods into me the moment his lips press against mine, until I'm full to bursting and glowing from head to toe.

He wants me.

And it doesn't scare me half as much as I thought it would, having Carter's attention focused entirely on me.

I didn't think I'd be able to handle it. Not after the last few years, anyway.

After enough time accepting that the spotlight will never

be yours, it almost hurts to find yourself caught in the light again.

It was only ever my job to give attention. Never to get it.

Garth used to expect me to suck him off during his boring late-night business calls. I cherished the memory of that one time he *didn't* roll over and go to sleep the moment he hung up—when he stayed awake long enough to give me orders on exactly how to jerk off.

I used to think that was the hottest it would get. But now that I'm touching the sun's surface, I realize I was living through a fucking ice age.

Carter kisses me slowly and tentatively, exploring my lips like he's trying to find the best way to fit them against his. Every way he tries feels equally perfect to me.

When he finally pulls away, I whimper a protest and tip my chin up.

"Is this okay?" Carter murmurs.

There it is again—that warm, deep voice I heard for a moment in the hallway downstairs.

I never even knew I *could* imagine him talking to me this way. I haven't heard it before—not in all the locker room interviews, underwear photo shoots, behind-the-scenes videos I've ever skimmed through for glimpses of him.

It feels like I'm being let into a brand new treasure chest of all his closest secrets, and I just want to kiss every single precious jewel.

I try to stretch onto my toes to close the gap between us again. But he's just a little too tall, and he's lifting his chin away like he's trying to listen to me. I can't overcome the distance. I'm too wobbly on my feet, because my legs—no, my whole body—is still shaking.

It hasn't stopped since I first wrapped my arms around him.

Maybe it's the comedown from my panic and stress, or the rush of being pulled out of the hole of self-pity I dug myself. Or the thrill of my deepest-held fantasies coming true at last.

Or I'm just fucking freezing cold from the ocean.

Carter gazes steadily at me, waiting for an answer. My throat feels thick and tight. It just stings all over again, realizing how strange it feels to be the object of someone's worry but not his pity.

"I will be if you kiss me again," I plead, widening my eyes at him.

My jeans are still painfully tight. Every kiss, every touch, makes me throb in them a little harder. I don't need a break—I need *more*, and soon.

Carter smiles and cups my cheek in one big hand, his thumb stroking my cheekbone gently to soothe away any anxiety about him changing his mind. "And I will," he whispers.

He's saying something else, too. His lips are moving, but I can't hear it.

I'm too caught up in the feeling of just one hand on me. There's this rush of electric sparks running down my spine at the way Carter combs his fingers through my hair, his nails running along my scalp.

His other hand rests on my lower back, just a little bit too low to be gentlemanly, and it's driving me insane.

God, I want to purr… or curl up in a ball in his lap… or maybe climb him like a fucking tree…

Decades of barely-repressed desire are bursting out all at once. No wonder I'm feeling half-wild.

"Mmmm," I whimper with a hopeful little stare. *Hope he wasn't expecting any answers. Is it kissing time again?*

Carter smiles fondly, sweetly, even a little bit surprised, but genuine to the core. "Oh, Fox," he murmurs, relenting and pressing his lips against mine briefly.

Yes! *Now* he's speaking my language, and I could die happy.

"Did you get a word of that?" Carter whispers, and then he carefully kisses me again.

"Mm-mm," I grunt, shaking my head before I press upward into the next kiss, dragging my tongue carefully along his lower lip.

Carter's breath turns rough in his throat, and I swear I feel his nails dig into my shoulder a little harder. But he pulls away from me again anyway, his lips just an inch away as he presses his forehead against mine.

"Let me sum it up," he murmurs. "Shower?"

Ugh. That's right. I almost forgot about my goddamn impending hypothermia.

What's the worst that could happen? Pneumonia? Nothing compared to the fact I'm going to *literally* die if my harbour dip cockblocks me at the very last possible moment.

But if I'm all warm and wet and naked... surely that will put him in the mood, right? And maybe it *is* a bad sign if I can't stop shaking.

Fuck, fuck, fuck.

I want to dissolve into a puddle of angst on the floor... but he's right. I need a shower.

"Yeah, yeah," I sigh.

"Yeah?" Carter murmurs, biting his lip. "Only if you want, of course."

Something's up.

My downstairs brain is in charge of the show right now, but something makes me pause before I answer.

Wait. My upstairs brain just joined the party.

He means we could shower *together*.

I pull back to look him in the eye, and then I lose my breath all over again.

Carter's looking at me in a way that steals the words right from my tongue. How can I possibly talk while trying to memorize an expression I've never seen before?

It's this shy, tentative hope, like he isn't sure I'll say yes.

I never imagined that.

The Carter of my dreams was forceful, confident, suave. Exactly the kind of guy I thought I wanted. But now I know the truth about those men, thank God Carter isn't just that.

I let my fingertips run down his sides—those muscled sides I know way too well, right to the V-shaped cum gutters—and grin at him like an idiot. "Uh, *yes*."

Carter flashes me a grin and takes me by the hand to lead me down the hall.

The part of me that wants to race ahead in my excitement and start stripping down so we don't waste a second is surprisingly small.

It pales in comparison to my desire to match whatever pace Carter sets—whatever he needs to feel comfortable.

So long as I'm here by his side, that's what matters.

CHAPTER *Seven*

FELIX

I haven't stopped trembling. If anything, the excitement is making it worse. With no manual dexterity, my soaking wet clothes might as well be glued to my body.

Carter is leaning into the shower to turn it on. If I weren't so desperate to feel his bare skin against mine, I'd walk into the shower fully clothed.

"Come on," I groan with a half-hearted shove at the hem of my T-shirt. "Work with me."

Carter turns to me and smiles. "Let me."

"Sorry," I mumble as Carter steps so close to me that I can feel his warm breath on my cheek.

"For what?" he asks, grabbing my hands. "This is *my* present. I didn't say you're allowed to unwrap it."

My mouth falls open.

That was kind of bossy, more than a little sexy... and, let's face it, cheesy as fuck. I can't believe he actually said it. But... Jesus, does it ever work on me.

Carter sidles closer, bumps into me, and doesn't stop. I

swallow hard, backing up as he pushes me right against the bathroom wall.

Then he eases his fingers right under the hem of my shirt and peels it up and off in one smooth motion.

"Oof!" The sudden, cold dampness against my shoulders and face—pretty much my only dry body parts right now—makes me gasp. But Carter makes it as fast as possible, like ripping off a band-aid.

Instantly, I feel better... and a whole lot hotter.

Carter tosses my shirt in the sink and runs his palms from my stomach right up to my shoulders, then down my back.

Wherever he touches, my skin sparks to life and keeps on burning.

"Oh, fuck," I gasp when his palm grazes across my nipple on the way to my shoulder.

Carter pauses, grins, and dips his head. His hot breath ghosts across my nipple, and then he runs his tongue around it, and I make some unholy noise as I clutch the counter behind me for dear life.

"Oh, I like *that* play," Carter chuckles, his breath a warm tease against the mix of cool and suddenly hot skin. "I'll remember it."

God almighty, he's not even just taking what he wants... he's studying me. And I *like* it.

Carter straightens up and runs his thumbs across my waistband. "These next, hm?"

"Nnnhyeah," I manage around my gasps for breath.

Carter laughs, and once again, he works his magical thumb magic to peel open my jeans, slide down the zipper, and wiggle them down off my thighs. And he even catches my soaking wet underwear at the same time.

Which means... everything hits the floor with a wet sound.

I bite my lip, suddenly nervous, and bend over to pick up my clothes and add them to the sink. I don't want Carter hurting himself doing it... and I'm feeling a little bit shy.

But when I straighten up, that's it. There's no hiding how turned on I am.

I'm naked, and my arousal is completely on display. Despite the equivalent of an hour-long cold shower, my cock is rock-hard and lying flat against my stomach.

Carter pulls away to better look me up and down... and then he smirks. "*My* present."

And I thought I couldn't get any harder.

But I don't think I've *ever* dared fantasize about what just happened.

He called me... his. Oh fuck fuck fuck don't cum on the spot...

I clench my thighs hard, and my cock jumps against my stomach.

Carter chuckles, catching his own shirt much more casually and yanking it over his head. He tosses it on the ground.

He's *gorgeous*. I barely even want to touch him, like I'm afraid he's a mirage that will melt away.

Within seconds, his jeans are off, too, and the only thing left is his underwear.

I thought my lips were moving silently, but a strangled, "Fuck," just emerged from the depths of my soul.

It's not a trick of the light. This is the exact brand Carter was wearing in my favourite commercial. *The pair*, in fact... my very favourite. And boy, there's a reason that shoot is infamous among the fans... even those who know nothing about hockey, like me.

They're tight boxer briefs, this perfect shade of pale blue that showcases his bulge more than anything.

It always looks like they can barely contain him.

But unlike the photo I could describe with my eyes closed… they're *really* barely containing him.

His dick is a hard line straining toward me, pulling his underwear away from his legs at the sides.

My brain comes to a grinding halt, until all I can focus on is the hard length between his legs.

"They usually fit better," Carter chuckles.

I gulp. "I know," I whisper back, and then I flush from head to toe with embarrassment at his startled glance.

Oh, man. Now is so not the time to admit to my Carter Haywood YouTube playlist.

"I mean, any boner's hard to hide. But, um… you've got a pretty big problem," I giggle weakly, hoping to distract him.

Carter lights up, just like I was hoping, and grins right back at me. "Yeah? You wanna see how big my problems get?"

"*Please*. Your problems sure beat mine."

"For the record, I like yours, too," Carter murmurs.

I'm tingling with pleasure, and finally starting to relax about all of this. Carter's seen me naked and he hasn't changed his mind or decided this experiment needs to be over.

"We're still talking about hard-ons, right? Not my huge pile of *actual* problems?"

Carter laughs again—a fond, warm tone that makes me buzz with happiness from head to toe.

But I can't tear my eyes off his bulge. The head is clearly pressed against the tent of fabric. The poor thing is awkwardly curved, obviously trapped by the fabric, and I wince in sympathy.

My hands slide down my stomach, but I can't quite bring myself to reach out for him.

Carter presses one hand on either side of me on the counter and nods down at himself. "Go for it."

"Well. If I'm invited…"

I'm doing it. I've definitely had this exact dream before, but it's actually happening.

I grab the elastic waistband, pulling them down across his cum gutters and muscled thighs…

The only difference is the small red scar on his hip—but I can't focus on that when I'm seeing him naked for the first time.

"Yeah?" Carter murmurs. He grabs me by the waist and spins me around until my back is to the shower.

"Yes," I gasp, catching my balance and getting ready.

He backs me toward the shower, but this time is even better. Every time he presses against me, his cock bumps mine, and a little shiver works its way down my spine. "You sure?" he teases me, his eyes glinting playfully.

"Yes!" I stumble into the hot stream of water, and he pushes me straight through it, up against the cool tile water.

Carter slides a thigh between my knees and rests one broad forearm against the wall, getting himself comfortable. Then he gives a little sigh and opens his eyes to slowly look me up and down.

Like he's planning what he's about to do to me—and he's got a hell of a menu to choose from.

"*Yes*," I whisper, even though he didn't ask again.

His eyes pin me to the spot. I bite my lip and shiver

against the cool tiles as they slowly warm up, but it feels like I'm burning up under his gaze.

Oh, fuck.

I don't know what's about to happen… but the balance of this best-worst day of my life is swinging pretty hard into *best*.

"What do you want?" Carter asks, and the growl in his voice makes me catch my breath with delight.

There's only one possible answer.

"I want you."

CHAPTER Eight
FELIX

I can't help it.

He still seems a little bit like a fantasy that will burst as soon as he's touched... I need to do it. And his broad shoulders and firm muscles are, to my utter delight, *real*.

All of him is real. From the hard dick pressing insistently against my stomach to the hot breath against my shoulder as he kisses a trail behind my ear all the way to my collarbone and nipple, then up my throat to my lips.

I'm on fire.

And it's not just in my palms. The salt water has rinsed away from my palms now, but the fresh cuts sting like *hell*.

I keep hoping Carter won't notice my winces, but it doesn't take him long.

"Whoa," he whispers, gently taking my wrists. "No more of that." He firmly guides them both above my head and presses them there."

Holy shit yes. My lips part, and my vision turns foggy as my hard-on throbs against my belly. I keep my wrists exactly where they were put, squirming from head to toe.

Carter grins softly. "You like me taking over, don't you?"

"Yeah," I breathe out with a shy glance away. But Carter just takes hold of my chin in his gentle fingertips, and then he waits there until I catch my breath and finally look at him again.

"Good," Carter murmurs, pressing a gentle kiss on my lips. "Because you make me want to."

Then he presses close at a weird angle. It takes me a few moments to realize he's presenting me with his neck and shoulder so I can kiss his bare skin without hurting my hands.

Whoa. Bossy, sexy, cheesy, *and*... almost romantic. God, how does this man keep getting better than I dreamed?

My nose is filled with the masculine scent of him. It doesn't take me long to find a spot right below Carter's ear that makes him press harder against me and grunt.

Naturally, I exploit it ruthlessly, running the tip of my tongue in gentle circles, flicking it across the spot, then sucking and kissing it.

Carter's breath comes in rough pants against my shoulder. He keeps shifting from foot to foot like he can't help grinding his cock against my bare stomach—like he's too needy to stop himself.

I know the feeling.

It's no effort at all to remember the way water rivulets look cascading down the hard muscles and planes of Carter's body. I'm branded by the sight, marked forever—and I'd never want to go back on it.

Jesus. Carter's so strong.

His muscular thighs, his perfect ass, his back and shoulders and arms and... just *every* part of him.

If not for his hip, he could pick me up and fuck me

against the wall without even thinking twice. I bite my lip, my gaze turning down to his fresh scar. *I wish he didn't have them. But then... he wouldn't be here.*

So in truth, I just want to take away any bit of his pain that I can.

"Yes," I gasp when Carter shifts his weight and the line of his cock slides against mine.

Carter glances eagerly at me, and then he glances down and grins, putting two and two together. "You want me to?"

"Please," I whimper.

The syllable is barely out of my mouth before his hand presses around us both, squeezing me tight. I squirm against the wall, sliding through the ring of his fingers and against the ridge of his cock.

"Fuck," Carter groans. He shifts like he's figuring out how to grind against me, and I shake my head. I don't want to make this harder on him.

"Would you let me?"

Carter hesitates, but only for a few moments. Then he seems to remember what I said earlier—the way I want to be equals—and he just groans and yields.

Holy fuck. *This* is the only way I don't want to be equals—when he's pinning me to the wall with all of his weight.

"Yes," I gasp, throwing myself into a rhythm like I'm riding him. Apart from the fact that I want him stretching me open, filling me up, pounding me into the mattress...

I groan at the mental image, my body drawing tight already. "Fuck. Holy fuck, yes, Cart..."

"Fuck," Carter pants for breath. His fingers tighten around our swelling arousals. His teeth graze against my neck and shoulder, and the little white-hot bursts of pain make me whimper and press even harder into him.

I'm going to cum—*we're* going to cum... any moment now.

I don't want this to be over already. I feel like a man who's wandered the desert for a lifetime, finally stumbling into a lush, plentiful oasis. I can't cup my hands and drink fast enough from the springs of desire.

But on the other hand, I might lose my mind if I don't listen to my aching need—and soon.

I press my nose into his neck, my knees almost giving way as my whole body draws tight and quivering. Every muscle in my body feels like a taut string about to snap at once.

"I can't... I can't stop..." I whimper, rolling my head back against the wall.

Carter nips my throat and growls against my neck, "Cum. Cum for me, Fox. Let me see it all."

A ragged cry escapes from my parted lips as I arch against his body. My toes dig into the pools of water at our feet. The backs of my hands slide this way and that against the wall as every inch of my skin glows again with Carter's heat.

Holy fuck. I haven't been this on-edge in as long as I can remember—

"I can't stop it," Carter grunts, driving his hips forward. He's doubling the friction between our cocks. And I can't possibly handle both of us pushing against each other into the same tightness. "I'm going to cum, too. Holy shit! Fox... I'm almost..."

"Yes!" I gasp. "Please cum, please, yes..." I lose track of everything that isn't the drumbeat of my heart or the ragged gasps of Carter's breath against my skin, the squeeze and throb as I draw tight...

And then it happens, all at once and so hard that I can't even remember my name.

"Yes yes yes *yes*—"

"*Fuck*," Carter growls against my neck. He grabs my hip with one hand and my wrists with the other, his nails biting into my skin.

Both of us fall apart together, intermingling our pleasure until I can hardly tell which is mine and which is his. We're both shooting our loads at once, coating each other in the same joyous, unrestrained mess.

I don't know how long it takes before I can piece together my broken brain. It isn't just my chest filled with that glowing warmth now—it's the whole damn world.

I'm blinking against the shower water. Carter's hands are running gently over my body, lathering me up and rinsing me clean.

He already got what he wants... but he's still being so gentle.

"Hm?" I mumble under my breath. "I mean... wow..."

"Shh," Carter whispers, kissing the back of my shoulder and neck. "You're all good. Let me grab a towel."

I should be trying to do things for him, right? But... I breathe out a happy sigh and shake my head. This isn't the moment. Not when my thighs are jelly and my cheeks hurt from smiling.

I do manage to turn the shower water off and shuffle around to face him.

He's smiling as much as me—maybe even more. It's a grin I haven't seen in a long, long time. Not outside of the photos in the paper when he's celebrating a goal or a victory.

That joy looks *wonderful* on him.

"Here you are," Carter murmurs, wrapping a towel around my shoulders.

I catch the towel with one hand, and his hand with the other. He pauses and looks at me, waiting, and I can't figure out what I wanted to say.

There's only one thing to try.

"Thank you," I murmur, hoping he can hear all the meaning.

Thank you for making my dreams come true. Even if it's just this once.

Carter smiles, and then he gently tugs my hand upward until he presses his lips toward it, his eyes never leaving mine as my cheeks burn with pleasure. "I'd do anything for the anti-hypothermia cause. But this was my pleasure."

I laugh, and then instead of one of us supporting the other, we kind of end up leaning on each other to step out of the shower.

It feels… strangely right.

CHAPTER Nine

CARTER

"Come here," I tell Fox.

I might not know where everything is yet, but I have an "important stuff" box for a reason. Antibiotic ointment was almost the first thing I packed, even though I'm past the point of needing it.

You never know when you'll run into your best friend's little brother, all grown up, hot as hell, and full of layers you want to spend years growing to understand.

For example.

"Oh, I'm—I'll be okay. Thanks. The salt does wonders," Fox tries to mumble his way out of it. I just crinkle my brow and glare at him until he sighs and gives in. "Fine."

There's a secret little glow around him all of a sudden, and he definitely thinks I don't notice it.

Of course he likes being cared for. Who doesn't?

I never thought of myself as a Florence Nightingale, but apparently I'm not bad at this.

Another thing Fox doesn't seem to realize yet is how he almost tiptoes when he approaches me. I can't decide which of us is the deer, and which of us is the human slowly approaching the meadow to try to befriend it.

Maybe we're each a little bit of both.

"This will sting," I warn him, but I think I'm bracing myself more than he is. The idea of causing him pain, even for a moment, is almost unbearable.

But Fox offers his upturned palms to me without hesitation. That trusting, clear-eyed gaze turns to me, and the spark it lights ricochets through my body.

Jesus.

If this isn't what it feels like to be struck by lightning, I'll eat my helmet.

"It's okay," he murmurs. "I've had worse."

I jolt and stare at him, almost afraid to ask the question because of how furious I know I'll get.

My jaw is tightening anyway.

Has someone hurt him?

I don't care who it is or where they live—they're going to pay.

Fox stares at me, and then he does that adorable thing where he blushes right to the tip of his ears. "Only emotionally. Don't worry," he hurriedly adds.

I let out a breath, and with it, a sheepish laugh. "I wasn't. I mean, it's not like I was planning how to call my twenty best friends and beat someone up."

Fox laughs softly, and I see that pleased little look in his eyes again—the one that says he can't quite believe anyone is treating him this kindly.

The red-hot fury is subsiding, but a good chunk of my brain is still fizzing with anger. It might not have been physical, but he *has* been hurt. Probably in myriad small ways over years, each adding up to contribute to the whole.

I always thought my career path was a sudden, rough way to leave home. But I didn't appreciate until now how lucky I've been, getting raised by the men I grew up around in the game. I've had bad coaches, but I was able to write them off, because I knew what good coaches were like.

They did the exact opposite of whatever Fox has gone through. They made me believe good things about myself. And in turn, I started to believe I deserved the very best.

It didn't happen overnight, but over the course of years. One game review, one shouted sideline comment, one Christmas card at a time...

That's how love is supposed to work: slowly and steadily. So why do I keep feeling like this one afternoon could mean everything?

Maybe I'm just seeking something to replace what I've lost. Ouch.

Think less, Florence more.

I squirt ointment across my fingers and gently trace them across the scrapes and cuts on his hand, wincing every time he flinches. But Fox never pulls his hands away.

"Done," I murmur, turning his hands over to rest his fingers gently against my palms. I raise them to my face to kiss the backs of his fingers... and then I pause.

He's got a tan line around his left ring finger.

Most people would probably come to a very different conclusion, but I know Fox's heart. There's only one reason for this.

Duh.

Took me until now to remember getting that phone call from Alph. Must have been three years ago now—right in the middle of my first real breakout season.

He said his little brother had just got engaged to a real asshole. If I remember right, his exact words were, "I'll always stand by my little Flick... but man, I hate his fiancé."

It wasn't just Alph being protective. He was right.

"Oh, Fox," I murmur, and I press my lips to that pale ring enclosing his finger. It feels symbolic, like a ghost that hasn't quite faded. "I'm glad you're back."

Fox closes his eyes and shivers, swallowing back everything I wish I could steal from him and toss in the deepest, darkest ocean to never haunt him again. Then he swallows again, and his voice is thick when he finally speaks.

"Me too."

God. It makes *my* throat tighten too, and I don't exactly cry at the drop of a hat.

I want to know more, but I let him pull away and head from the en-suite into the bedroom. Like mine, Fox's pain is still a little too raw to look at for too long.

"You got anything my size, or am I gonna be streaking home?"

Now, there's a distracting thought.

"Uh..." I scratch the back of my head, ditching the towel on a bathroom hook as I follow him. "Maybe try the dresser. There's sweatpants. Help yourself to whatever fits."

Felix snorts as he digs through, rejecting most of what's in there at first glance. Finally, he finds a grey pair and holds them up. "These look smaller than the others, right?"

I cringe as I settle down to sit on the edge of the bed. From here, I can reach my box of whatever easy-wear clothing isn't in the dresser. "Technically, yeah."

Of course he found the oldest, rattiest sweatpants I own. I've only held onto them because they have my junior team logo on the thigh. I should have retired them to a mementos box or something.

But then, I didn't anticipate someone else digging through my clothes anytime soon.

It's weird to see Fox holding the grey material up against himself. Like he's slipping into the rest of my past, after I left Sunrise Island behind, to watch from the corners there, too.

But I like it.

Fox groans. "I don't have the ass for any of these."

"They'll just ride low at the front, won't they?" I grin. "I don't have a problem with it."

"Pervert," Fox gasps, his hand rising dramatically to his chest.

"Apparently," I laugh.

For everything else, he seems to have held onto that part of his spirit, and I'm so fucking glad. I've always admired the way he's unapologetically camp. Not quite femme, but not... *not* femme. Miles away from the masculine, rough-and-tough guys I'm around all day.

Huh. Maybe that's why I was never into anyone like this.

I've always been a little curious about the other guys. Maybe a little horny from proximity to all the horny parties and sweaty, testosterone-filled post-game showers.

But now? I mean, I can't stop staring at Fox's narrow back and the subtle curve of his triceps as he leans over the dresser to dig through the T-shirts.

I tug a pair of loose sweatpants on and grab a shirt myself, but nothing distracts me from the fact that Fox isn't wearing anything underneath my old sweatpants. I'm even having these crazy thoughts about... *sniffing* them later, when he gives them back.

Who the hell am I?

Come on, Cart. Knock it off.

There's stuff we have to talk about before we get down and dirty again.

If my suspicions are right, I'm gonna hear things I never wanted to hear. But he's the one who had them actually happen. The best thing I can do now is just listen.

So far, Fox is just about the only person to ask the questions others are afraid to—and still not treat me like I'm a delicate glass ornament. I just hope I've learned enough to do the same for him in return.

"So, that guy in... Vancouver, wasn't it?" My mouth is dry. I swallow past it and finish my question. "How long ago was that?"

My life is defined by the strictest measurements of time—critical seconds that can mean winning or losing a game, or even a whole season.

But the silence after my question is the longest few seconds of my life.

CHAPTER Ten

CARTER

Stay cool and wait.

I want to apologize and back down, but something in my gut tells me that wouldn't be the right thing to do.

I need Fox to know that I know—and that it's okay.

He wants me to open up, but I need him to do the same thing. So far, he's managed to go this whole afternoon without breathing a word about it. Even though his scars aren't physical as mine, the impact of his own collision with fate is just as clearly visible to me.

"You really want to know?" Fox asks softly.

"I do." I lean forward, fidgeting with the tie of my sweatpants. "Anything you want to share."

At last, Fox is looking at me over his shoulder.

There it is again. The ghost that's been haunting him, whose shape becomes more and more obvious as I put the pieces of this puzzle together.

But I keep my mouth shut and wait.

At last, he sighs, and I could almost collapse with relief.

I haven't pissed him off for good.

"We were together a little over five years," he tells me. "He proposed two years in. And... I finally came to my senses a couple of weeks ago."

Whoa.

I whistle under my breath. "That's not long."

Does that make me a rebound? I don't know a lot about this stuff personally, but I hear enough from my buddies. Some of them have gotten burned pretty badly that way.

"Yeah. He flew to some beach resort and told me I'd have to leave when he got back." Fox bites his lip like there's more. But then he shakes his head, standing a little straighter like he's already realized it doesn't matter, and he's letting it go.

Colour me impressed. I know a lot of players who could learn from that attitude.

"How are you dealing with it?" I ask.

Fox chuckles. "Pretty well, actually. But I'm not surprised."

"Yeah?"

Maybe I'm not a rebound, then... no. Quit it.

I furrow my brow, wrestling all that hope into a box in my brain and put it away, the way I do my anxiety before face-offs. Before I can be anything else to Fox, I have to be his friend and listen to him. Not the selfish voice in my head, however loud it is.

"I mean, he was an asshole for years." Fox laughs. "Just took until now to notice. I can be pretty good at lying to myself. World-class, in fact. I've got awards and everything."

Huh. He doesn't sound as sad as I expected—at least, until that last part. That's when the humour kicked in. The deflection attempt doesn't stop me noticing his shoulders sinking as he grimaces through the words.

"We all do it sometimes," I offer gently. "We cope however we gotta cope."

Maybe I should have waited until he was within hugging distance.

Fox finally settles on a plain white T-shirt, and he pulls it on over his head. It's huge on him, but somehow he still looks hot. It's like every ripple of fabric teases a hidden line of his body.

He pulls at the fabric, and then he smiles a little bit and looks at me.

"That's it. It feels like I've been shrinking for years. Getting smaller under this… this great weight. But it's melted away, and I can breathe."

"Yeah. I can see it on you."

And boy, is it a relief.

"Maybe it's just being back here. Sure beats the Vancouver smog," Fox laughs.

My eyebrows fly up as my brain grinds to a halt. "You were… in Vancouver?"

That's where I lived—when I wasn't on the road, of course. *Lived? Live?* I still own my bachelor pad there, emptied by the movers of everything but furniture and a few changes of clothes.

"Garth wouldn't be anywhere else," Fox rolls his eyes. "He thinks it's the centre of the world. Richmond's basically the prairies."

I snort with laughter. But it's a small, forced sound. Underneath, my fury is cold as ice spraying from a steel blade.

Fox was so close by.

Fuck.

If only I'd known he was so unhappy.

COLLIDE

Why didn't I pay more attention to Alph when he told me the news? I know exactly why. I was too caught up in myself and my stratospheric rise from promising prospect to star player.

This island always felt like a time "before the game," even though that's not really true. I could skate backwards before I could write cursive.

But whenever I wasn't at school or on the ice, I spent every minute of my spare time with my friends. So much time—and so much trouble—that the grownups started calling us the Sunrise Brothers.

Ouch.

There's a team I haven't thought about in a long time. For all I know, Alph and the others are still as close as ever. Meanwhile, I barely know where they're living. Certainly not what they're doing and how life's been treating them.

When did it happen?

When did I stop making trade-offs and just start sacrificing everything else that once mattered to me?

"I'm sorry he was such an asshole," I sigh, and it's only at the last minute I managed to say *he* and not *I*, which is what I really wanna say.

Fox would just get confused; he never expected me to look out for him. But I could have anyway.

I would have wanted to.

"I'm not," Fox says and shrugs. "Makes this easier. I mean, the hundred-whatever shoe boxes?" he waves vaguely toward the window. It's overlooking the backyard and not the driveway, but I get his meaning.

"Yeah?" I ask, my curiosity engaging. "I was wondering about them."

A bunch of guys I know like collecting shoes, but most of

them are straight hockey players. And I sure as hell didn't see many shoes in there.

I saw lots of other stuff, though.

Great. I'm blushing again.

"That's what he sent the rest of my stuff in."

My brow furrows. What does he mean, *sent the rest of his stuff?* I mean, surely he means exactly that. But I can't be getting it right.

Who the hell would be that much of a petty asshole?

Fox is waiting, an ironic smile lifting one corner of his lips. "Yeah, I know. Asshole."

"Wow," I breathe out, my jaw dropping as I stare at Fox and slowly shake my head. "I take back what I said before. If he sets foot on this island, I will *kick his ass.*"

Fox laughs and leans against the dresser, his arms folded. "Nah. He's too good for this place. I mean, when I left and moved in with him, it was like a fifteen-minute floatplane to the mainland, and he wouldn't come. I should have known who he'd turn out to be."

Now I *really* want to punch him. But at the same time, the anger is subsiding within me, like I'm letting go of the play-by-play and seeing the big picture.

"Thank God he did."

Fox blinks at me and then snorts. "That he turned out to be a massive dickhead?"

Shit. That doesn't sound right.

"No, no." I clear my throat and push myself to my feet. "For him realising he's not good enough for you."

Fox squints at me, but I frown right back at him and fold my arms.

I mean it.

A few moments pass, and then Fox's expression finally

relaxes. He settles into a rare, soft, full smile that I don't think I've ever seen before.

If I had, I'd remember it.

It's like the dark cloud has passed by, and the sunshine in his soul just switched on again. Suddenly he's breathtaking and beautiful—and then, in an instant, it's gone again.

I ache to bring it back. I *will* bring it back. Even if I have to walk the length of the Earth.

The only problem is, I don't know if he'll let me.

"So…" I murmur. "I guess we should talk about the plan?" I don't know how to start talking about this stuff except to just bring it up and hope for the best. There's no point in avoiding it.

Fox swallows hard. "For today? Or… for us?"

"Both." Maybe it'll be easier if we aren't standing in my bedroom, though. "Over coffee?" I add.

Fox groans like I've just promised him an all-day blowjob. "I'd love some. Thank you."

Shit. Absolutely stop thinking about giving him an all-day blowjob. I'm not wearing underwear, either.

"I'll meet you in the kitchen," I tell him as I rummage through my bedside table for my painkillers.

"Cool," Fox murmurs back. He hesitates for a moment before padding over to me and pressing his lips to my cheek.

If I wasn't blushing before, I am now. My heart's in my mouth, like it came at his simplest calling.

"What's that for?" I ask softly, my hand rising to cup his soft cheek. His skin feels so delicious under my thumb, but his lips are *right there*, so even though I should probably kiss him back on the cheek…

I duck my head and peck him right on the lips instead.

Fox blushes. "Everything," he whispers, and then he flees.

I stand there for way too long after he's gone, staring after him as a jumble of emotions takes hold of me.

Wow.

I've been body-checked a lot in my life—and it was only a life-changing disaster once.

But Fox has really got me good.

CHAPTER Eleven

FELIX

Holy shit.

I'm wearing Carter Haywood's spare clothes, standing in Carter Haywood's kitchen, and looking for Carter Haywood's coffee mugs.

And not because I'm a creepy stalker who broke into his house and licked all his stuff—and I definitely haven't had any fantasies about that. No, sir.

I just had the hottest sex of my life. With Carter Haywood.

All my fantasies are coming true. True, except the ones about him shoving his dick in my mouth... but if I'm very, *very* lucky, I might get the chance to make that happen.

It all depends what Carter wants. And right now, I couldn't begin to guess.

I've never heard any speculation about his sexuality. All I ever heard—or really, tried to avoid—were the headlines. And boy, are there plenty of those.

The rumours are fast and furious about him. Famously, he never confirms any speculation about his love life. But he's had lots of pretty models on his arm at lots of fancy parties.

It's obviously not a problem that I'm... well, a guy. Carter came just as hard as I did in the shower—maybe even harder. But what if he's having second thoughts now?

I guess I'm about to find out. Hopefully faster than I can find these goddamn mugs.

"They've gotta be *somewhere*, right?" I've run out of cupboards to try, and I don't want to rummage in boxes yet. I tug open a cutlery drawer, then the one below it.

There they are—all neatly lined up in rows.

"Ugh. Really?"

I can't believe I've spent my life crushing on a guy who keeps his mugs in *drawers.*

By the time I hear Carter's footsteps, I've got the fancy coffee pods in the fancy coffee maker. It's got way more buttons than anything I've ever brewed coffee in, so I feel pretty damn successful.

It's almost enough to make up for the sickening anxiety that's been steadily building in my stomach.

I brush my fingers against my lips, closing my eyes as I remember the taste of Carter's soft kiss on my way out of the room.

That has to count for something.

I know Carter's different. This won't be the kind of "let's sit down for a talk" where he complains about things I did, and if I say diddly-squat about him, he makes it all about me, too.

"You found everything." Carter smiles at me as he comes around the corner. The pride in his eyes just at this tiny achievement chases away the last of those shadows in a heartbeat.

"Despite the odds," I snort.

He slowly strolls past me to the kitchen island. The stools are high enough that it doesn't take much to sit on them, but he pauses on the way for an anxious glance at the coffee pod box. "Which ones did you use?"

"Timmy's."

"You star," Carter sighs.

I have to laugh. The only other kind he has are fancy caramel things, and he had a tiny dusty box of them shoved at the bottom of this one. It would take real effort to guess wrong.

"I just guessed you were out there living the stereotype." I grab a stool and pull it under the island to the other side, then plop my ass on it as the smell of coffee starts to waft through the air.

"Hey now," he protests. "There's nothing like it. When I'm on the road…"

Then he trails off and shakes his head like it doesn't matter.

But he's not fooling me. He's still trying to figure out what happens now that his future might not look like he always thought it would.

I know the feeling.

"Anyway, the plan?" I prompt him gently, to take his mind off it. "The rest of my stuff will be at the ramp now. Murph said he'd drop it off." I bite my lip. "I guess we can't take Frog *or* the wagon I, uh… borrowed."

Shit. Once I figure out whose it is, I'll have to do more than bake a pie. Will they take a pie-a-week deal?

Carter just grins. "No problem. Let's see what I can do."

Oh, no.

My cheeks burn as I catch my breath, ready to protest.

This isn't how I wanted to come home. I could have walked to any old neighbour and asked to borrow their golf cart...

But I had too much pride. After years letting Garth call the shots, meekly following in his shadow, I wanted to feel like I'm doing it myself.

Too late. Carter's already chatting to Murph like it's old times, asking who's still around, taking down phone numbers.

I pinch the bridge of my nose and stand up. If all I can do is pour the coffee while everyone else solves the real problems... well, I've got years of on-the-job experience.

I don't like moping around. But this just feels a little too much like old times.

The memory's rising from deep in my bones. Hours spent sitting on the stairs down to the TV lounge until my ass went numb, listening to the cool kids.

Carter, Alph, Murph, Zach, Drew...

I can still hear Alph when he found me. It always the same: "Flick! Mind your own frigging business, huh?"

Then the game was on. Sometimes I took off fast enough to avoid it, but usually he'd catch me and flick his fingers against my ear. It's funny, even affectionate, when he does it now but it annoyed the crap out of me back then.

If one of the others came upstairs to go to the kitchen or bathroom and stumbled on me, they'd roll their eyes and holler, "Alph! Your kid brother's here again." Even Murph had a particular groan that meant pretty much the same thing.

Carter was the only one who always kept his mouth shut. He just teased me by ruffling his knuckles through my hair on the way past.

It's not like I've *never* had friends. There were a few other kids around our age—mostly girls. We got along well, but we lost touch as soon as we no longer had ferry trips to and from high school.

But I always wanted brothers. Not a big brother like Alph, but a group of friends to stick with me through thick and thin. I've never really had *a* friend like that, let alone a whole group.

I make Carter's coffee the way I remember him liking it—a little cream, no sugar—and I take my time stirring creamer into my own. By the time I sit down again with the coffee cups, he's done with his calls.

"So—" he starts, tossing his phone on the counter, and then he glances down with surprise. "Cream, no sugar?"

"Yeah."

He blinks and looks up at me, a little wrinkle appearing between his brow like he can't quite believe his eyes.

I just shrug. Remembering people's orders always comes easy to me. Garth used to joke that if I left him, I could always work at McDonald's.

Okay, that's a lot more asshole-y now that I'm thinking about it.

"Thanks," Carter says, then clears his throat. "So Zach's home. His golf cart *isn't* a well-disguised torture device, so it actually runs. He'll pick up Drew in an hour or so, and they'll drop off everything in your driveway. That all right?"

Well, now I'm speechless.

And I feel kind of like an idiot for moping around and wishing I had friends.

Sure, maybe they're just doing Carter a favour. But they're still doing way more than they have to, and it makes me feel a lot less like I'm sitting on the basement stairs.

How many ways can I get exactly what I always wanted in just one day?

"That's... really nice of everyone. Thanks."

Carter beams and shrugs, then sips his coffee and closes his eyes like it's the best thing he's ever tasted.

It would be enough to turn me on if I didn't still have one thing nibbling at me.

"How'd you hear about me and Garth?"

"Huh?" Carter looks at me, then shakes his head. "Oh. Alph mentioned it a few years ago."

Years ago? I thought it'd be a lot more recent. Like when Garth missed my birthday dinner, and it was blatantly obvious to everyone but me that this was going off the rails.

But the fact he remembers anything about me when he's been off living this big, exciting life... it's kind of amazing to me.

"Speaking of which," Carter says, sitting up a little straighter as he wraps his palms around his cup. "I guess we should have that part of the talk."

"About... Alph?"

"No," Carter stops and shakes his head. "Sort of, yeah? I mean, Alph's gonna kill me, isn't he?"

I scratch my chin as I try to figure out a way to soften the blow. But I distinctly remember the glares he used to give Garth whenever the two men's paths crossed. He's got "overprotective older brother" down to a tee.

"Okay, maybe. But you've got a fighting chance."

Carter snorts. "Thanks. At least he's living—where was he again? Edmonton?"

Oh, shit. I thought the two of them still talked regularly, and I haven't told him.

I kind of wish this conversation had happened after the conversation I was expecting—the one about us.

But there's no way of ducking out of it now.

"Uh... he was, yeah. But there's another reason I moved back here," I tell him. "Not just the free housing." He raises his eyebrow and gestures with his mug for me to go on.

Ugh. It sounds kind of pathetic, but I can't think of any other way to say it.

"I didn't want to be alone."

Carter gives me a little sympathetic smile for just a moment—long enough that I know he gets what I mean, but short enough that it doesn't make me feel like shit.

Then he laughs. "You sure picked the right place. Smart cookie. It should be our official tourist slogan: *You're never alone on Sunrise Island*."

I burst out laughing, nearly spilling my coffee.

Information travels fast here, and gossip travels faster. Even after years away, I bet we'll be able to write a biography of any of the island's residents by next week.

"I mean, yeah," I tell him when my giggles finally slow down. "But that's not what I meant. I mean... Alph's moving home, too."

The look on Carter's face makes me almost want to laugh again. There's a strangled look of worry for a moment, and then delight, and then a return to the worry.

"And he won't kill you," I add, watching his expression balance out into cautious optimism. "Probably."

Carter slowly shakes his head, and finally the delighted grin returns. "All the brothers back again. How cool is that?"

I flinch slightly, because I've just gotten a peek into Carter's life that I don't think could have happened back then. He used to be too wrapped up in the other four guys' lives, and vice versa.

This doesn't mean he'll forget about me, does it?

Whoa. Don't get so clingy. Nobody's promised anything yet.

"Where's he moving to?"

"Mom and Dad's place, same as me." Carter gives me a disbelieving stare, and I shake my head. "What?"

"So we're all going to be neighbours?"

"Oh." I squint. "Technically, yeah." There's no houses between ours, just lots of trees, so I didn't think about that until now.

Shiiiit.

What if I misread all of this? What if he's only now realising that we'll be in each other's proximity every day for the foreseeable future? That's what it means to hook up with someone else on Sunrise. It's a big responsibility.

"It's... it's not a bad thing, right?" I ask hesitantly.

Carter clears his throat and shakes his head. "Uh, no. No, it's cool. It's just... if Alph's living with you, too... it'll get out. If we keep—assuming you want to keep doing this—" he breaks off, fidgeting like hell with his coffee cup. "Do you?"

I flinch as it sinks in.

Of course. He doesn't want to tell anyone about us.

That makes a lot of sense, actually.

I take a deep breath and reach across the island to take his hand. "I do," I tell him softly.

"Even if I want to keep it secret?" Carter presses me.

"Yeah."

He doesn't need to know that him wanting to keep exploring this with me is... I can't even describe it.

It's like an entire choir of angels just descended from the

clouds and told me that an all-you-can-eat ice cream cart will follow me around for the rest of my days.

Maybe even better, and that's saying something.

What's he thinking? I squeeze Carter's hand and he lets me, but he doesn't return it yet.

"It's not that I'm ashamed or anything," Carter tells me. His brow is still furrowed. "I don't want you to think that."

"I get it."

I should have expected it, really. I don't know a lot about sports, but I know the blessing of Carter's career path has come with the curse of all the media attention he no doubt hates.

And I'm not exactly front-page material.

"I can keep my mouth shut," I promise him. "Especially here."

The slightest hint of us being an *us* will set the island on fire with gossip. But I don't need everyone to know about it. I've got nothing to prove anymore.

"Okay," Carter breathes out with a sigh of relief, and he finally squeezes my hand. "Thank you for being cool about it."

"And you want this to continue too, right?" He sort of said it, but I want to hear it out loud.

Carter looks like I'm asking him to confirm the sky is blue, and I gotta admit, that helps with all my worries. "Uh... yeah."

"Okay," I tell him, and I can't stop the grin that spreads across my face. He lights up in his own smile like he's echoing me, and for a moment, everything feels...

Peaceful.

Carter leans across the kitchen counter, setting down his

mug to cup my cheek in one warm palm like he wants to kiss me.

I can practically hear the swelling romantic music. I almost lean in automatically... but then I pause.

Carter opens his eyes and blinks at me, but I'm even more startled.

In all my fantasies, I've always been so desperate for his touch that I'd do anything he tells me to, bend to the slightest whim.

But this is real life, and I'm finally learning the lessons I should have all those years ago.

"I've got a rule, too," I tell him, squeezing his hand firmly.

"What's that?"

"No strings," I tell him. "No hearts getting broken. This is just... fun, between friends. Friends with benefits, if you like."

A thoughtful crease appears in his forehead, and he watches me closely, his hand unmoving on my cheek.

As if he's never had anyone make this offer before. I can lie to myself, but not quite that far.

I hold my breath, the seconds tick by, and then Carter lets out his breath and runs his thumb along my cheekbone.

"Okay," he murmurs and gives me that big, boyish smile again. "That's fair."

"Any more rules?" I ask.

His eyes twinkle mischievously, and he leans in to whisper his answer against my lips. "If this is fun, why limit it?"

And honestly, I couldn't agree more. Go big or go home.

No, wait. It's different for us.

Go big *and* go home.

CHAPTER
Twelve

CARTER

WHAT. A. DAY.

I can't see it from here, but on the other side of the island, the sun is meandering down the horizon at its lazy spring pace. Soon, it'll light up the trees in pink and orange, and the waves between the harbour and our island in shades of gold.

The dog walkers and neighbours out for a stroll prefer that side, but there's nowhere I'd rather be than Brothers' Cove.

Well, it's more of a series of boulders that curves around gently, giving the illusion of a cove when you're sitting down in just the right nook. That's where I am right now: firmly settled down with a beer in one hand and back against the rocks.

This was always my favourite place to come. *Our* favourite place, I should say. Nobody calls it Brothers' Cove but us. We liked to imagine it was our little secret.

I've only been back for a few days, but I'm glad I finally made it here.

If anywhere's home... this is it.

In all the chaos and rush that my life's become, if I ever needed to find a calm place inside... all I had to do was close my eyes and think about this spot.

It's just like I remember.

If I roll my head back, I can see the arbutus grove behind me. The trees are a little older and taller than I remember, but I've changed a lot more than they have.

Ahead of me, waves rhythmically lap against the pebble shoreline. The tide is going out, and tiny birds skitter around each newly-revealed rock pool. Once in a while, I spot the distinctive grey lump of a seal breaking the water and slowly rotating before it vanishes again.

Most of Sunrise Island's beaches overlook the other islands, or Vancouver Island—as we call it, the mainland. The actual mainland and Vancouver itself is somewhere way in the distance ahead of me, barely a mirage on the clearest of days.

So why, if I'm surrounded by all this nature, do I feel like a thousand butterflies are chewing their way out of my stomach?

I'm a million miles from anywhere, but I can't escape my own head.

"God," I breathe out softly. "What's wrong with me?"

I know the answer. And *wrong* isn't quite the word. But it's new and different and pretty damn huge, all things considered.

Fox.

I can't stop thinking about him. All afternoon, since he left. He was too stubborn to let me walk him home, but he did text to say our friends had dropped off all the boxes like they promised.

I knew they'd come through. Or I hoped like hell,

anyway. After all this time away, they were good about letting me call in one more favour.

Anything to help Fox.

Poor guy had the moving day from hell, where mine was perfect. I bought my new place with last year's bonus and arranged the movers before I was even out of the hospital. All the hard stuff was done by the time I flew here.

Ha. Hard stuff.

I'm right back to thinking about this afternoon's *literal* hard stuff, and how fucking hot that shower was.

I'll admit it: I've jerked off a couple times this afternoon to the memory, and even *that* is a hundred times better than my usual half-hearted attempts to imagine myself with some faceless stranger.

Now I have a face, a name, and a sinfully beautiful pair of lips to put to the fantasy, and it's *so* much better.

Whoa. Not here, Cart.

I swallow a groan as I raise the mouth of my bottle to my lips for another swig.

Whenever I wondered why there was nobody in my life, why I blanked every girl who clearly wanted me to ask her out...

Well, I wasn't kidding when I told Fox that we all lie to ourselves sometimes.

I told myself I was too focused on the game until everyone else started believing it too. *That Cart—don't bother. He's a heartbreaker. Too married to the game to notice anyone else.*

Now I'm like, stop number one for hot models who want a paparazzi shot and a networking opportunity. They love knowing I'll be a gentleman; I love going home early.

But that all feels like... *before.*

I can't believe what's changed in the last few hours. A

whole lifetime not knowing what I was missing out on. All because of Fox's green eyes and bright smile and beautiful soul.

And it sounds like this is just the beginning.

Should I be worried about it? Is this just lust, a fleeting attraction that will vanish tomorrow?

No. I'm not worried, except when I try to make myself feel worried.

And it's not just about the new feelings in my pants—as welcome as they are. I'm always at stupid fancy parties posing for pictures with stupid fancy people, and not one of them has ever caught my eye like this.

And every other part of me, too.

There's no getting around it. Fox makes me think faster, try harder, and want more. I feel different around him. More like the *me* I feel like when I'm alone, only...

I'm not alone.

"You out here drinking by yourself?"

The holler almost makes me jump out of my skin.

"Jesus!" I yelp, grabbing at my beer bottle before it tips over in the gravel.

"Thought so," he answers, and now I can place it: Zach's voice. Asshole.

Footsteps crunch on the gravel nearby, and someone else shakes a very rattly plastic bag. "Without so much as a bag of Doritos?" Definitely Drew.

"You make low-carb sound like a bad thing," I grumble as Zach and Drew poke their heads around the edges of the rock. "And drinking alone."

Murph brings up the rear. As always, he doesn't say much, but he raises his eyebrow pointedly.

Zach groans and says what they're all thinking.

"Because they're both signs that you need an intervention."

"And here it is. Also, the Doritos were two-for-one last week." Drew plops down next to me and flings an arm around me. "Hey, buddy. It's been years!"

"Yeah, it has—" I start to try to form an apology, but they won't let me get a word in edgewise.

"Look at you. Man, you got ripped." Drew eyes me and then looks down at himself. "Maybe I can meet you halfway on the carbs. Is spaghetti carbs?"

I laugh helplessly as Zach squeezes in on my other side. "More beer?" Zach throws his backpack on the pebbles with a thud and joins us, half-hugging me and slapping my back. "I brought a six-pack."

"And then some." Murph sets two tote bags down and groans, sinking into the gravel. He has to sit kind of sideways. We've all grown up and filled out so much that there's less room than there used to be.

"Doritos!" Drew shakes them with a cheerful grin.

Zach tries to grab the bag from his hands. "Stop breaking the chips, you idiot."

Just like that, it's like no time has passed. My face just about splits open in a grin.

"I'm not breaking them!" Drew elbows him and tears open the bag. "Look, they're—uh. Well, there's still good ones. On top, see?"

"I'm confiscating the rest of them," Zach grumbles.

"Anyway, I'm providing a valuable service. An auditory tasting menu, if you will," Drew insists.

I snort with laughter. "Nerd."

"Mega-nerd," Zach agrees, and Murph shrugs as he grabs for the Doritos.

Drew rolls his eyes at me. "Don't pretend like your mouth isn't watering over him."

I freeze. *Shit. Did they figure it out? Who else knows?* But I try to play it cool. "Over…?"

"Yeah, yeah, play innocent. Wait 'til you see the dressing. I know you're a slut for them."

Duh.

Of course he said *them*, not *him*.

Fuck. What's the opposite of a Freudian slip? A Freudian leap? Whatever it is, I just did that… but my secret is safe.

"Yeah," I laugh with the sudden relief, a little too loud. "Yeah, you know. Not allowed that shit in training. Carbs, you know. But now…"

Do they know? Am I going to have to tell them? God, I don't want to bring down the mood.

Murph nudges my knee gently with his elbow and then reaches for a beer to crack it open. When I look at Zach and Drew, I can already tell—they know.

Phew.

The breath rushes out of my lungs, and Zach finishes my sentence for me. "Now, school's out!"

I join in the laughter with the rest of them. He's not wrong. It does feel kinda like the first day of summer.

"And we're almost reunited. I heard Alph's back soon."

Zach beams at me. "Next week. I'm gonna take the boat over and help with some stuff, if you wanna—" he pauses, then grimaces. "I mean, if you wanna say hi."

"It's okay. I can lift," I tell him. "And walk. Just not very fast. Getting better, though."

They all nod, but just like Fox, they don't dwell on it.

"Good," Drew speaks for them all. "You know if you need anything, we gotcha."

"You all really helped out today," I tell them, raising my beer bottle to clink against theirs in thanks. After I sip, I shrug. "Other than that, uh…"

I wish I could talk to them about the one thing I *do* need advice on.

Zach's fooled around with guys for sure. Nobody from the island, as far as I know—that's just playing with fire—but let's just say he's been to drama camp. Back then, Drew was just as quiet as me on the love life front. And Murph... well, he's quiet about everything.

It's ironic that Alph's my best bet… if only it weren't for the thorny little brother problem.

"I'm good for now," I finish up. "Thanks, guys." I let that sit out there for a moment, and then I grin. "Now cut the BS and tell me what's up before I die of old age."

I'm really glad they're here. For a few hours, maybe I can stop thinking about me and Fox. Where we've been, where we're going, our goddamn rules…

And whether I'm about to make the biggest mistake of my life.

CHAPTER
Thirteen

FELIX

A few days later, I still haven't recovered from the emotional whiplash of the best and worst day of my life.

It's almost weird how I haven't spontaneously run into Carter yet, actually. Not at the mailbox, or the grocery store, or even in his front yard whenever I walk past.

But I'm not afraid that he's ghosting me. He texted the next day to ask if I wanted to meet by the wharf for coffee—this time, my choice and not out of a pod.

That means in public.

The coffee shop down by the wharf tries much too hard to have indoor seating. It's jammed right in between what's probably the world's smallest grocery store, and the world's smallest fire station.

There are three tables inside, each with two chairs. When it's raining too much to open the takeout window and you can't get past the tables, whoever's sitting down has to pass down your coffee like a relay race.

Basically… even compared to the rest of the island, it's impossible not to be overheard.

And Carter's text? Well, I told him the usual. *That would be great, I'll let you know*, and a bunch of sparkling emojis.

He gave me a thumbs-up, and since then... radio silence.

Of course I want to see him. Even if it *does* feel like a test of how discreet I'm really willing—or able—to be.

It's just been busy, that's all. There's so much to take care of when you're moving house—especially when you aren't moving into a household that's already been set up, albeit by an asshole. You know how it goes. Utility bills, groceries, that old island tradition of missing the ferry and spending the hour catching up with everyone you see...

"This would be easier with a boat."

Unfortunately, until I find a real job—for the first time since Garth and I got engaged—the boat I'm staring at is the only one going.

Our old family boat is nowhere near the water anymore. It's in my backyard, and I'm staring at it through chest-height weeds. The trailer wheels are half-buried in the dirt. There are wildflowers growing so high that I can see them from my eye level—which is below the boat's edge.

That's not even mentioning the holes.

"I mean, we must be able to seal it up—" I prod carefully at one jagged hole. Something metallic flakes away from the hull, and I yelp and jump away like it burned me. "Shit. Was that paint or... or *boat*?"

This is way beyond my DIY abilities. I'll have to leave it for Alph when he gets here next week.

Apart from that, it's starting to feel like a home again. *My* home, I should say, because the first few days back in my childhood home were distinctly weird.

When I'm not daydreaming of Carter Haywood feeling

me up under the table at the island coffee shop, I'm wandering around, just… daydreaming.

I thought it would be hard to picture a whole new future here after so long staring down the barrel of the glossy, fake future that Garth offered me. Turns out, compared to trying to make myself *want* that future… this is easy.

On the boat front, though, I admit defeat.

"Fine. I know my domain."

I head back inside and tug the screen door to make sure it's closed, then wander around the side of the house to the front.

It would feel weird to take the shortcut through the basement now that it's no longer a TV lounge. My parents turned it into a self-contained suite when they made this place their vacation home. Last winter, they decided they didn't want to fly out here and deal with "island politics" every summer.

It's like it was meant to be. As much as your life falling apart can ever be *meant to be*, that is.

Alph called dibs on the suite, and I don't mind. I prefer the house. It's bigger, even if it's older and a little tired. I like the familiarity. I know which floorboards creak and which cupboard doors have to be wrestled open.

As soon as I stop walking into the office—once my childhood bedroom—I'll be good to go.

But I'm not headed for either my huge new domain of the master bedroom *or* my old turf right now.

I'm going to Alph's room, which now the guest room… and right now, shoebox storage central.

Amongst all the cobweb clearing and family heirloom herding, that's the one thing I haven't been doing: unpacking. Mainly because every time I look at this *disaster*, I get overwhelmed.

Nothing is grouped together. They were obviously packed purely by size. Luckily I didn't have any furniture, because I'm pretty sure he would have ground it into sawdust just to make his little stunt work.

The biggest things I had were my winter coats, obviously packed in vacuum storage bags in the three shoeboxes that are wrapped completely in tape and bulging every which way.

I groan before I even push the door open, and the exact same sight confronts me as always.

"God, what a mess."

But... I can't keep running from this. Both from my stuff, and from what I really need to do.

I have to text Garth.

I've started to write that text, like, a hundred times now. I kept deleting it, worrying about whether I should rise to the bait. I know he's just waiting gleefully to find out how mad he made me.

But this isn't for his sake—it's for mine.

And maybe... just maybe... Carter's.

"Okay," I tell myself aloud, raising my phone to tap out a message. "We're doing this."

I didn't find that prank funny, Garth. Boxes arrived safely anyway. Let me know if anything else is outstanding. Otherwise, I wish you well and hope you're treated better than you treated me.

Before I can overthink it and delete it again, I hit send and shove my phone in my pocket.

I expected to have a lot of feelings, but the tidal wave swamps me: surprise, ferocity, and more than anything, pride.

I finally stood up to Garth.

This has been a long time coming. It can't all be from one afternoon, however great it was.

But my heart feels full of a warm confidence that doesn't feel like it came from me. And I know one person who walks around every day radiating the exact same feeling that's been glowing in my chest for several days.

I have one more text to send before I chicken out.

How's this afternoon? Coffee and a walk on the beach?

Without giving myself time to think, I send it. Then I nearly drop my phone.

There are three dots! Already!

Perfect. Pick you up at 3?

I clap a hand over my mouth to muffle my squeak. I'd do both hands if I could, but I'm clutching the other phone to reread the message until it's burned into my brain.

After these last few days, it feels like something is bursting free... and it might just be me.

What's a cool, casual way to respond that doesn't sound frosty?

I can do 3! I add the emoji with three little hearts floating around it, then delete it. That might be coming on too strong for a friend with benefits. I try the blushing cheeks emoji instead. Yeah. That's better.

Three dots. Pause. My heart leaps into my throat. Three dots again—there it goes, and—

See you then. x

I stumble into my room—the right room this time—and drop my phone on the bed just before I collapse onto it myself.

Even if I had someone to tell about this, and I could, they'd never believe it.

I'm going on a date... even if it's just a friends-with-benefits date... with Carter Haywood. And he's picking me up from my house at three o'clock.

And he said... *x*.

What's that? Is it a hugging x? Or a kissing x? Or a *I'm too cool to sign my name because I do a hundred autographs every other Saturday so I just go with this* x?

"A hug," I decide aloud. It sounds cool and confident but also a tiny bit flirty. I know what his hugs feel like. It's just enough to make me remember the feeling of his hard body pressed up against mine.

If I play my cards right I might just get to enjoy the *not-safe-for-the-public* version today, too.

Speaking of which, what am I wearing? Shit. That's a riddle if I've ever heard of one. It has to be lightweight for summer, but dressy enough for date, but also casual enough to be like, *hey, this isn't a romantic thing, it just has some of the best features of romance.*

Also, tight enough to look hot, but not like I'm *trying* to look hot.

But if anyone can find a solution, it's me.

I bounce right back onto my feet and stride to the guest room. There's no question about it. I'm *going* to seduce Carter, and all the outrageous remnants of my past couldn't possibly stand in my way.

CHAPTER Fourteen

FELIX

At the first sound of the doorbell, I skid across the hardwood floor to answer it.

I haven't had a date in... years, really. I can't count any of Garth's bullshit make-up attempts as dates. Not that *this* is a date. It's coffee with a friends-with-lots-of-benefits.

And I can still be excited about it.

"Hi!" I exclaim as I yank open the door, a grin already spreading across my face.

Wait.

It's not Carter standing there.

It's Berty Baker—president of the Sunrise Island Residents' Association. AKA, the guy who cheerfully loaned me the golf cart I managed to wreck without even getting behind the wheel.

Shit.

"Oh—oh, hi, Berty! Uh—how's it going? Nice to see you. Sorry," I stutter. "I wasn't expecting company. I mean, uh... you."

What are the magic words to make a chasm open and swallow me whole?

"Hey, Felix!" Berty greets me with a broad smile as he leans on my porch railing. He's wearing both his trademarks—a horrific Hawaiian shirt, and a huge grin. "The culprit himself!"

I groan, clutching to the side of the door as I thump my forehead on it. "Oh, God. It's about Frog."

Berty's laugh is just the right balance of amusement and sympathy to make me not feel any worse about my great return to the island. His notoriously laidback attitude is why he's been president for five terms in a row.

His husband Doug is just as nice as Berty, but otherwise his exact opposite in fashion sense—as in, he *has* one—and extroversion. I swear he gets around the island by teleportation, or else sneaking through the woods.

"Don't worry, kid. It looks worse than it is," he promises me as I straighten up and look at him again. "Mostly bodywork damage, and Drew can hammer that out in no time."

I can't quite escape my cringe. "Really?"

"Yeah, yeah," he waves his hand. "I'm just glad all you boys are coming home. And Carter's right next door, huh?" He gestures in the direction of his house, then folds his arms and grins like he's in on the secret.

I'm pretty sure he isn't. But if I flinch now, he *will* be, so I carefully wrestle my face into just the right casual smile. "Yeah. It's nice to know my neighbours."

"The Sunrise Brothers are back together!" Berty laughs loudly.

Wait. He's just... casually including me in the cool kids' gang, and it makes me feel like a fraud. I open my mouth to protest, but I can't really get a word in edgewise.

"Oh, it's been dull around here since you all grew up. We need more kids here. But now the next generation is moving back, huh? Settling down? Sunrise is a great place to raise kids."

Oh, my God.

"Uh—I don't have a—I mean, it's not really the right time yet…" I stutter, my cheeks burning.

Berty waves off the details. "Doug and me, we had our babies thirty years ago." He snorts. "But they never left home. Should have thought that one through."

Even I have to laugh.

Thirty years ago, he and his husband Doug started both Sunrise Island's only restaurant and bar and a ferry service to get mainland tourists here. They used to do it all themselves—driving the ferry, serving guests, and cooking.

Nowadays, Berty just spends his days talking everyone's ear off. Including mine.

The clock is ticking, and Carter is due any minute now.

Hopefully he sees Berty's golf cart outside and realizes I've got company. Otherwise, things could get awkward in a hurry.

"That kind of baby, maybe I could handle," I manage, my cheeks burning. "If I knew what I could do. I'll think about it."

"You'll figure it out," Berty says with way more confidence than I deserve. "And stop by anytime if you want advice. And at least a business won't eat you out of house and home!"

Oh, shit. That reminds me.

"Pie!" I exclaim, pointing at Berty. "I have pie."

Berty points back at me. "Sounds like you got yourself a great lunch, kid."

"No, no—I mean, for you—" I fumble with the front door, gesturing for him to step inside. "Let me just run and grab it!"

"Don't worry about it," Berty beams, but I can see the interested gleam in his eye. He steps inside, leaning on the door instead of the porch railing. "Incidentally... what kind of pie?"

"Blueberry." I know it's his favourite. I sidle back toward the kitchen and press my palms together with a pleading look. "Please, Berty. Take the pie for Doug?"

He's still being polite, making interested but noncommittal noises. "You sure? If this is about Frog, you've got nothing to worry about."

"No. Well, yes. I made apology pies. And now I have *so many* pies."

"Wellll..." Berty drawls, and I light up with a hopeful smile. He's starting to give in. "How many pies?"

"Uh..." I blush and scratch the back of my neck. "I panicked, so... four."

"Four?!" Berty laughs. "Well, all right, then. But you come over for dinner soon, all right?"

"Great," I breathe out and scurry for the kitchen.

I don't think that's how an apology is supposed to work, but it's about right for Sunrise Island. And I'll take their home cooking any day of the week.

"Who the heck are they all for? A block party?" he calls out. "Oh, oh! I got it—you can start a pie business!"

He wouldn't be saying that if he knew how many I started with.

I snort as I grab the box of tin foil to cover up the pie tin. "One's for me and C—"

Wait. Shit. Is that breaking the rule?

Or is it weirder to avoid mentioning me and Carter

hanging out? No. Berty might be the nicest guy on the island, but he talks to *everyone*. I'll just cross my fingers that Berty didn't hear that over the crinkle of foil.

"—And, uh, one's for Drew, for fixing up Frog. The third's for the owner of the, er… the other vehicle involved in the accident. And the fourth is for you, for my sins."

His hum is long and meaningful.

Shit. Is he figuring it out? No way. I haven't given him anywhere near enough clues. Unless he's seen or heard something…

Wow. My part of this secret is nothing compared to Carter's, but it's still so stressful. Ironically, I'm an expert at sneaking around, but not *this* kind.

"Okay. Pie."

When I approach the front hall with the wrapped-up pie, he's giving me a meaningful grin that makes my heart jump into my throat.

"What if I told you…"

Oh, God. Don't drop the pie, whatever he says.

"The wagon was mine?"

I almost drop the pie anyway. He sees and lurches forward, but I recover it just in time.

"Fuck. I mean, uh—" I stutter, blushing.

Berty laughs like he doesn't mind me swearing. It just feels weird when he saw me growing up, you know? "How about you give Alph the other one when he gets here?"

I open my mouth to protest that he won't be here for another week. But if I'm not careful, we're going to get into a politeness deadlock and he'll still be here when Carter shows up, all dressed like he's about to take me out on a date.

That would burn up our rulebook in a hurry.

"Okay. Deal. Thanks, Berty," I steer him outside by grabbing the door again. "Thanks for stopping by. And let me know about the wagon. I'll replace it, of course."

Berty pauses, and then he looks at me thoughtfully. "Hey. I just had a thought. How about a deal, instead?"

"Yeah...?" I venture. I can't drive a ferry, and I definitely can't cook a crisp fish fillet. Surely he knows *that*, though.

"This year's Strawberry Tea," he says. "It's a disaster. Our planner backed out, and the committee can't agree on a single thing."

"Isn't it, like, a week away?" My hand rises to my mouth. I can picture it now: no cake, too much tea, and an eye-watering combination of design choices.

I might not be a baker, but that doesn't sound like a recipe for a successful fundraiser.

Berty's trademark smile fizzles out. He actually looks *stressed*. "Yeah. Nine days. We wanted to expand the playground this year, too."

He mentioned a deal, but I don't hear one coming yet. Unless... I narrow my eyes. "You want... *me* to help? How? I've never been on a committee."

"No, no," Berty reassures me. "I'm talking about hiring you as the new planner."

I blink at him a few times. "Huh?"

"If we don't get a pro, they'll just keep voting on frosting colours all day long." Berty shakes his head. "We need someone we can count on—someone who knows how to throw a party."

Huh. I never thought anyone would pay me just to be a good host. But Garth *did* count on me to do all that stuff. At one point I was planning an event a week—dinners for his friends, parties for his business clients. And, okay, once or twice, a charity fundraiser.

Nothing as important as a Sunrise Island Strawberry Tea, though.

"Ah." I can't argue with that. In fact, the more I think about it, the more I like the idea. "Well..."

"This could be your new business!"

If I don't take this, God knows what he'll try to persuade me to take up. Boatbuilding, maybe.

"You know what? Yeah. I'll do it." It'll keep me distracted from thinking about Carter 24/7, but I'm *not* telling him that. "It'll help me, uh... live down the shame."

Berty grins. "Ah, could be worse. You could have crashed Ladybird into your mailbox the night before the golf cart parade."

It's a damn good thing the pie isn't in my hands anymore.

"*What?*" My jaw drops.

Berty just winks at me and strides down the porch stairs. "Glad you're home, kid. Next time you need anything, you just call. Or knock," he turns to tell me. "You know how it goes here."

Actually, I'm not sure I know up from down right now.

"Yeah," I call after him. "Thanks, Berty."

"And think about businesses!" Berty calls out before starting up the golf cart to drive off, pie balanced in his lap for safekeeping.

I will. In fact, he has no idea just how much he's given me to think about.

CHAPTER Fifteen

FELIX

I DON'T KNOW WHAT I WAS EXPECTING TO SHOW UP OUTSIDE my house at the appointed hour... but it wasn't a brand-new golf cart.

Especially not *this* cart, which doesn't look like any I've seen around before.

Either he's turned the usual hierarchy upside-down, or...

"Did you just import... *is* that a...?" I trail off helplessly and gesture at it. I don't know nearly enough about cars, but it looks kind of like a classic car had a baby with a golf cart.

Carter grins sheepishly. "I swear it's all by the book. It just *looks* like a '57 Chevy."

"You're not a smuggler now," I breathe a sigh of relief, clutching my chest as I hurry down the path toward him. "I can be seen with you in public. Thank God."

I pause just as I reach my front gate.

Oh. Oops. That was a little close to home.

Carter doesn't seem to notice, though. "I'll show you all the bells and whistles later. Wanna go for a ride?"

"Hell, yeah." I almost bang the gate on my shins in my haste to close it.

"Oh." He looks me up and down, then blushes as he glances at his pale blue jeans and crisply pressed, yellow checked shirt over a white T-shirt. "Wow. I feel underdressed."

"No, no. You look good." I don't need to say out loud that the way he wears the sleeves rolled up is perfect, but I can't stop staring at his forearms.

"No. Shit. *You* look good. Really good. Sorry. I, uh—I should have started by saying that."

Carter's getting all flustered, which makes me hide a grin. Exactly what I intended.

Outfit success.

I went with short, cream-coloured linen pants rolled up a little to make them into capris, brown leather sandals, and a white linen shirt—worn unbuttoned pretty low. Great big sunglasses hooked around the top button, of course.

...Maybe it's a little overdressed for Sunrise Island. But it's not *that* weird for me.

"I gotta dress up if I want to ride in this." I pat the side of the golf cart. The convertible hood is folded down behind the white and turquoise seats. I can't help but grin, the more I look at it.

Carter blushes and rubs the back of his neck. "It *is* a little too much, isn't it? I kinda impulsively bought it after... you know."

Now I'm joining in the blushing party. My hapless homicide victim, Frog, is currently hidden away in Carter's garage. Drew is the island's best golf cart mechanic, but he's fully booked this week.

This ride is way nicer, though.

I climb up onto the bouncy seats and grab the side handle, peering over the tinted windscreen. I think this is my favourite vehicle of any variety I've ever been in.

"You got this in like, three days? I can't believe it."

Carter chuckles, sounding embarrassed. "I paid several people a stupid amount to get it here."

"Hey. You need a way to get around if you're gonna be back here," I tell him, touching his knee for a moment.

I want him to know it's okay. I'm not going to judge him for an impulse buy. Especially when I get to ride with him.

And ride him? Fingers crossed.

"Yeah," Carter laughs as gravel crunches under us and he sets off. It's so quiet, I can barely believe it. "Now I'm all set to get my mail."

Oh, shit.

I feel like an idiot. I turn on the seat to face him. "Hey. Is that why I haven't seen you the last couple of days?"

"Well… you know. Surgeons said I pushed it too much. Told me to rest a bit," Carter says to the road ahead of us. He's wearing big, round aviator sunglasses so I can't see his face.

Duh.

"It's okay," Carter starts.

"No," I tell him, sternly poking him in the chest with one finger. "If you've been sitting there surviving on microwave meals, not getting your mail, while I'm right next door…"

He slows down for a moment, casting me a startled glance before he looks back at the road. "It's okay. It was only a couple of days."

"I should have thought." I shake my head and sit back on the seat, frowning at the road.

I really overestimated how much he can walk around right now, and then... I just plain didn't think.

Carter slows down as he approaches the corner, reaching out for a furtive squeeze of my thigh before he lets go again. "No, really. Don't feel bad. I wanted to give you space... if you needed it, I mean. To think. About, you know. Everything."

"Everything, like...?" I tilt my head up at him.

"Us," Carter says softly. He casts me a few anxious sideways glances. "I mean, if that's still..."

I laugh, glancing at the houses we're passing by. With no sight of anyone outside or on the road, I risk a little brush of my fingers down his forearm. "Does this outfit not tell you *it's still*?"

Carter laughs sheepishly and looks me up and down again—while we're still moving.

"Pothole!" I grab the wheel and haul it toward me just in time. The cart lurches, throwing me against his side, but I'm just in time.

"Shit." He grabs the wheel to hold on, and then he starts laughing. "Shit. Sorry."

I grin, my chest swelling with satisfaction. "That's not a bad compliment, you know."

"Uh, yeah. But I think I'm not gonna look at you until we get there. Just in case."

God, I don't know why I spent these last few days worrying about anything at all.

It's just so *easy* being near Carter... so right. The only problem is making sure I'm not *too* near him.

Honestly, I don't see that problem getting better anytime soon. But that's the only problem, really.

If everything else is perfect... what do we have to lose?

I'm not surprised that Carter's golf cart turns heads and attracts comments all the way to the coffee shop. I'm just glad he manages to extricate us from each ensuing chat in under five minutes flat.

And *very* glad that we don't run into Berty on the way.

"How do you do that?" I marvel as he parks in the little parking lot by the wharf.

"Do what?"

"Get out of conversations with, you know… the grownups."

Carter laughs. "We're grownups too, now," he reminds me, and then he makes a little gesture like he's about to take my hand.

My heart lurches. I fold my arms casually while he leans into the golf cart and takes the keys out, then puts both hands in his pockets.

"I guess so," I finally answer him. "But man, those are transferable skills on your resume."

It's barely two minutes before we reach the coffee shop—and thankfully, the takeout window is open today.

Carter leans in to order and pay for us, and I thank him, and then we head away from the handful of people who are always around at this time of day.

We might not be alone on the beach, but at least there's a lot fewer people, and a lot more to look at than inside the coffee shop.

"This was a great idea," Carter grins at me, keeping his coffee balanced. "Way better than sitting inside."

Then he very gingerly hops over a ghostly-smooth driftwood stick. He pumps his fist like it was a log, and I applaud against the back of my hand, because to a guy recovering from hip surgery, it probably felt like one.

"Yeah," I agree. "Sitting inside is all fun and games until your news is all over the island. Or worse still, you're passing eight coffees to Crooked Jim and his poker buddies."

We share a laugh at the ridiculous moments we call normal, and then we lapse into silence. I blow on my coffee, trying to cool it down to drinking temperature.

"I missed it here," Carter admits after a minute, giving up and putting the lid back on. He comes to a halt and sighs, pausing for a full turn to scan the whole horizon before he looks back at me. "A lot more than I knew."

"Yeah?" I pause, my feet shifting around in the pebbles underfoot, and look at him. "The neighbourhood drama?"

"No," Carter chuckles. "The… it's such a stereotype, isn't it? The laidback pace of life. It's like, half a myth, and half true."

"It *is* true," I have to agree. "Just like all the nice people."

He laughs. "Those are more real than mythical, though."

"Yeah." I gingerly slurp the foam from the top of my coffee. "That's the part I missed the most."

Carter winces sympathetically at me. "Yeah. I bet," he says, and then he reaches for my hand—again.

We're further apart, so his hand is almost halfway between us by the time he freezes. "Uh…" He slowly turns his palm up to scratch his neck, grinning sheepishly.

"Sorry."

Oh. Oh, man. He isn't worried about people seeing us, which means he's thinking about my rule, isn't he? "Hey. Look," I tell him, trying not to sound like my heart is fluttering in my throat. "Just because of my rule, it doesn't mean you can't be… you know…"

He raises his brows and stops walking to turn and look at me. "Be what?"

The hope in his voice is so plain that it gives me a little bit more courage.

"A little romantic...?" I test out the word before working my lip between my teeth. "I-I'm not *against* romance. I'm just not giving my heart away again like that."

Carter nods slowly. "Ever?"

Whoa.

That's the question, isn't it? But... ouch.

"Sorry," he whispers. This time, he does take my hand and squeeze it for a good couple of seconds before letting go. "I know it's all pretty new."

I clear my throat. "No, it's... it's fair to ask. I just don't know."

Carter nods, and then he reaches out to cup my cheek. "I just want you to be okay. At the end of the day... that's the most important thing."

That helps me let out my breath again and smile at him, and he meets me with a smile, too.

When he finally drops his hand from my cheek, he smiles again.

"We couldn't have done that at the coffee shop, either."

"Ah." I hesitate, and he raises his brows, so I clear my throat. "While we're being emotionally raw, I guess I should keep going."

Carter nods eagerly, and I fidget with the coffee cup. I don't want to say anything to shatter that peace, but... that's how it started last time.

And that means being honest.

"I wondered whether meeting at the coffee shop was, um... a test," I admit.

Carter stares blankly at me. I won't lie, that's kind of a relief. He's not the kind of guy who could have hid that reaction.

"You know, about how discreet I can be."

Carter shakes his head, still clueless. "Go on."

"Well... everyone here knows I'm gay. They always have. And I can't pretend to be straight—even if I *could* pretend..."

"Oh my God." Carter sucks in a quick breath and takes my shoulder, stepping close to me. "Fox. No, I never want you to think—that wasn't what I meant with my rule. Not at all."

A spot of tension I didn't even know I was carrying seems to unwind at his words. "Yeah?" I whisper. "Sorry. It's just one of those passing moments."

Carter shakes his head. "Be yourself. Wherever you are, whoever's around. I mean it."

I lick my lips and offer him a little smile, and he finally gives me one more squeeze and lets go.

But as we set off walking again, I can't help but wonder.

What if myself is impossible to separate from how I feel about you? How I've always felt about you?

No matter what he asks of me, it feels like I'm going to have to hide something.

But that's my problem... same as it's always been.

CHAPTER
Sixteen
CARTER

I like walking on the beach with Fox.

We have to go pretty damn slow for my sake, but it means we get to talk a lot more deeply.

Even if he doesn't want to get his heart involved, I'm so glad he'll let me stray close to him in an emotional moment.

This time when we set off walking again, we're just close enough together that our spare hands brush together.

Maybe I'm orchestrating it slightly by carrying the coffee in my left hand, not my right… but Fox doesn't have to know that.

"So you hate fancy mansions and elbow room, right?" Fox quips.

"What?" I laugh. I'm not sure where he's going for this, but I'm prepared to be roasted a little. I think I've earned it several times over with my custom-ordered electric Chevy replica golf cart. "I'm not exactly living in a tiny home."

"Well, you could be getting groceries delivered to your Vancouver penthouse. But you're about to join the morning rush for fresh milk."

Whoa. I'm only getting one thing from that, and it's delightful. "They sell milk now?" I exclaim. "I need more, actually…"

Is that a rude way to end a date? For that matter, is this a date? Every time seeing Fox raises even more questions.

"It was new last summer. My parents called me about it," Fox laughs. "But it's first-come, first-served and the first ferry brings it over."

"Oh. They don't have a fridge?" I blush before the question's even out of my mouth.

"In the world's smallest grocery store, no, they don't," Fox teases me with a straight face.

I raise my coffee cup and point it at him. "I'll bet you there's a vending machine out there somewhere that technically counts as a grocery store."

"Only on a technicality. Face it. Sunrise Groceries is the size of a shoebox—and I'm an expert, so you can't argue," Fox says with a grin.

Whoa.

I can't believe he's able to joke about that already. It startles me into a laugh, and then he grins at me all smugly and my heart just melts.

I've never seen that look on his face… but it suits him beautifully.

And it makes my brain stop in its tracks, so I couldn't argue back even if I wanted to.

"Okay," I agree, swaying toward him with my next steps. "I'll let you play that card."

"I think that card comes with unlimited lifetime play," Fox tells me.

"No, yeah. You're good."

After a minute, my mind drifts back to the beginning of the conversation, and I glance at him.

Is he trying to ask if I miss that lifestyle? That's a rant I'm more than happy to go on with him.

"I hate the whole sideshow," I tell him. "The press tours and the behind-the-scenes bullshit where we have to like, play these personas…"

I just wanted to be a guy who plays hockey the best I possibly can. I put up with the rest of it so I can do that. But when they want me to be someone else, I put my foot down.

The idea that, however briefly, Fox thought I wanted him to be anyone other than himself… it's horrifying.

"Yeah," Fox grimaces. "I don't follow the headlines much, but… it doesn't look fun."

I shrug. "The parties are fun, though. Not the crazy rich person, tower of champagne, caviar and ballgown ones. I check out of those early. The ones where my nice buddies make low-key embarrassing idiots of themselves."

Fox laughs. "Like what?"

"Well, uh…" I cast around in my mind for an example that doesn't make them sound *too* idiotic, and then I laugh. "Like when they don't realize that the hot tub is filled with wine—"

"Gonna come back to that one," Fox mutters under his breath, making me pause for a snort of laughter.

"—and jump in fully-clothed. Yeah. Okay, that's not a crazy rich person one, I swear. It was two-buck chuck. And it was a bet," I hastily start to explain.

Fox raises a hand. "I don't need details," he promises, and then he smiles. "I'm just glad to hear about it from your point of view. The headlines all made you sound like you were…"

"Standard rich, spoiled hockey kid?" I half-smile at him.

That's the downside of cultivating the image that, weirdly enough, keeps the press most off my back.

Fox gives me an apologetic little smile. "I guess."

"I don't mind. You can say it. Some of the guys do get lost in the real wild parties," I admit. "But at the top level… you still gotta be able to show up and play. That forces work-life balance." I tip my hand from side to side. "Sort of."

Felix shakes his head. "I'd take any of those parties over any of mine."

"Well, shit. I know a good party planner?" I offer, hoping to cheer him up.

Instead, Fox bites his lip and looks up at me with wide eyes. "Um… Garth made me plan them. And by the way, I'm kind of the new planner for the Strawberry Tea this year."

Ohhh, shit.

Awkward.

I practically fall over my feet, and my tongue. "I mean, there's the other ingredient. The even bigger one." Fox's eyes only get wider, a little more pitiful, and I groan. "The guests! Shitty guests, shitty time. Right? That's gotta be it."

Finally, Fox can't stop his grin from cracking through, and I let my breath out and shove his shoulder gently. "You asshole. I thought you were mad at me."

He giggles softly. And I swear, that noise makes up for at least a year of possible pranks.

"Smart move, using the shovel I've handed you," he teases me. "I'll bail you out. You're right, actually. Finance bros."

I wince. I can't imagine anyone who'd get along worse with Fox. Apart from like, axe murderers and the obvious bad party guests. "Seriously?"

"Yep. I can't talk *shit* with them. All they know are stock trackers. I tried everything. Eventually, I just got really good at… creating an aesthetic and refilling drinks," he waves a hand.

God, he has *so* much more to offer than that. Yet again, I swallow back the urge to fly to Vancouver, track down Garth myself, and pop him right in the nose.

He lost Fox. That's enough punishment for one lifetime.

We're reaching the other side of this point, and the trail back up to the parking lot.

"Your Strawberry Tea will get the whole island talking," I predict with all the genuine confidence I feel in him.

"We'll see." Then Fox looks thoughtful. He looks at me like he wants to say something, but he isn't quite sure how.

"Spit it out."

"If I had a guest of honour…"

I grin at him, already three steps ahead. "So I'll call my publicist. She'll put the word out with the people she knows—"

"Whoa. Whoa, you mean… you'll do it?"

I shrug. "Of course?"

Fox shakes his head. "But… you hate that stuff."

"Nah." I smile at him. "I only hate it when it's pointless. This has a point."

"Huh." Fox thoughtfully looks away, and then he offers his arm to steady me on the climb back up. "Thank you."

When we reach the top, I stop in my tracks as it occurs to me.

I know what else he needs, besides a job to keep him busy.

"Hey, I've got an idea."

"Uh huh," Fox says warily, but he smiles.

"Would you wanna come to one of mine sometime?" I hastily add, "Not one I'm planning. But one of the guys. Levine always does one around the end of the season."

Fox is staring at me like a deer in the headlights.

Shit.

"It's, like, *the* event of the year. For me, I mean. It's not like a red carpet thing. Buddies-only. People bring their wives or girlfriends... or, you know, their best friends..."

Technically it's true. It's just that most of the guys will at least have a girlfriend of the week they can bring along. Only the hardcore bachelors like me bring along friends.

"Sometimes siblings. That can get dicey, though," I pull a face and draw my thumb across my throat. "A lot of flirting when the booze comes out."

It works. Felix finally snaps out of his little pale-cheeked trance and laughs. "Right, okay, I just..."

"Uh huh?" I walk slowly with him toward the golf cart. If only I could kiss him, maybe I could distract him.

He'll be *perfect*. They're going to love him. His wry little sense of humour, the gentle way he listens to whatever you're interested in, even if he doesn't know much about it, and those little flashes of fierce sass...

He's the perfect host. He'll make a great guest, too.

"Really?" Fox asks. "Me? With you?" Then he blushes. "I mean, not *with*-with you, but... with you?"

"Why not?" I smile softly at him. "If you can mingle with those hoity-toity assholes, you can hang out with a bunch of my buds."

But he's just stopping, raising his eyebrows, pointedly looking himself up and down. Then he looks at me.

I wait and tilt my head.

He holds up his hand, and I almost take it before I realize he's showing me his nails. They're painted in a pale cream colour, like that fancy French kind.

"Wow. Nice. You do that yourself?"

He laughs like I'm being an enormous dumbass. "Yes, but —*Carter*."

"What?"

"Am I *really* gonna fit in there?"

Oh, shit. He means…

"Dude, trust me. Just be you. This version of you I've been getting to know."

Fox's face stays solemn, but this time I see the flicker of amusement in his eyes. "Which is different how?"

"Oh, no, mister," I grin. "I am *not* digging that hole again."

Fox giggles and swings himself up into the golf cart seat. "Fine. Busted."

"But seriously," I tell him, climbing up next to him. I pause before digging out my keys. "Trust me. They're all our age, you know? Some of them can be idiots, but at their heart —they're all cool with it."

I can feel Fox's tension melting away, and the hesitant excitement building now. "Really?"

"Really," I promise. Then I grin. "And the wives and girlfriends will love you. You're not competition." I lean in and lower my voice. "Or at least, they don't know it," I wink.

Fox laughs, and then he leans into my shoulder. "Okay, okay. Fine. You've twisted my arm."

I want to pick him up and spin him around for joy. But that's not really what friends do—even friends with benefits —is it?

Instead, I pump my fist in victory and bounce straight upright in the seat to reach in my pocket. When I've got the golf cart keys, I start it up with a cheerful whistle.

Fox is talking out loud like he's calming himself down. "I can figure out an outfit ahead of time. And you can give me a rundown on who's going to be there…"

I freeze, my hand on the parking brake, and then I clear my throat. "Oh. Yeah. Sure."

How do I break this news?

"I know that face." Fox glares suspiciously at me and folds his arms. "What?"

I wince, sticking my tongue between my lips for a moment, but there's no sugarcoating it. "Right. I didn't say that. The party's this weekend."

"Wha—" Fox makes a little strangled sound.

I press my lips together and give him the most apologetic look I can.

Fox looks away for a moment, and then he draws a breath. "Okay. But only because you're so…" he waves a hand in a circle at me. "Great big puppy, when you're excited."

I beam at him. "Puppy? I'll take puppy, if it works."

"It's working," he grumbles. "Drive me home."

"Yes, sir," I tease. "Should I pant at you?"

"*No*," he groans, and I laugh as I pull away.

"Thank you for trusting me, Fox. It'll be great. If you wanna hide away, we can find a corner of the yacht—"

He plugs his ears. "La la la *absolutely* stop talking before I change my miiind," he says in a singsong voice that makes me burst out laughing so hard I almost crash the golf cart.

Above all, I'm just glad he didn't ask the obvious question: *why do I want him there so badly?*

Maybe because the answer is just as obvious to me. Probably to both of us. Just… hopefully not to everyone else around us, too.

As we pull up in Fox's driveway, I cast him a hopeful little smile.

He smirks back at me, but then he hops out of the golf

cart. "I was going to invite you in, but it looks like I have more unpacking to do."

Goddamn.

I almost—*almost*—regret it... until Fox relents and smiles.

"Come over early before we leave for your party."

"Like, half an hour early...?"

Fox raises his eyebrows. Then he raises his coffee cup and slowly slurps down the last bit of foam, taking his sweet time about it.

Jesus on a cracker.

By the time he lowers it again, my cock is at half-mast and my mouth is hanging open, and my regrets have probably doubled.

"I *am* that good," he murmurs at me with a wink, "but I want to take my time."

I can't even guess at a time—not with my brain in this state.

"Make it an hour. Two, if you want to give an opinion on my apology pie."

"I'll make it two." I'm not going to turn down *more* time with him.

Fox giggles in that way that melts my heart. "I thought so. And thank you for today. I had a good time," he tells me.

Then he leans in and his soft, warm lips brush against my cheek, and my brain totally shuts off.

The moment he turns his back to walk down the front garden path, I raise my fingers to press them against that spot.

I have no idea how I'm going to make the drive home... but I have a very good idea how I'm going to spend my evening once I get there.

CHAPTER Seventeen

FELIX

I'M NEVER GOING TO ADMIT HOW MUCH OF TODAY I'VE SPENT trying on clothes.

I've already found the perfect black belt and shoes, and slim-fitting grey trousers that show off my ass. All I was missing was the shirt... but I think I've finally found the answer.

"Yes," I breathe out, tossing aside the socks that were stuffed into the box on top of the shirt. "This is it!"

The silky satin catching the light makes me hold my breath. It's a black floral print on white—sleek, thin, and silky. Perfect for a warm evening at a *casual yacht party*, which is a phrase I've never thought in my life. There's an oversized floppy collar, so it doesn't look like I'm trying to show up for a Hollywood red carpet.

But I also won't be totally out of place if a red carpet springs out of the bushes and surprises me.

It's one of the prettier things I own, and I forgot all about it. No need to wonder why: I bought it a couple of months ago, the last time I *almost* stood up for myself.

Garth shut me down by taking me to shop and get lunch together, all couple-y. When I came out of the dressing room wearing this shirt, Garth halfway glanced at me, gave an approving grunt, and stared back at his phone.

I saw on his face the moment he remembered he was spending the day masquerading as a human and not a flea-bitten dick stuffed into a human suit. Only then did he look up and coo something about how good I looked.

And I swallowed back all the red flags in my gut as usual.

I should've been shitting red flags for days. Or miles. However you want to measure it, a *lot* of them over the years.

But I guess I wasn't ready to face the truth.

"Scissors, scissors—aha!"

I snip the tags off and hold it up to the light, imagining myself standing next to Carter wearing this.

Wearing it tonight feels perfect. It's a reminder that I'm carrying forward the lessons from my last chapter, but starting anew. This time, Carter isn't the only one setting the rules.

No romance. No telling anyone.

I grin mischievously. *Good luck keeping your hands off me wearing this.*

All's fair in love and war, right? Or… not-love. Friends-with-long-dreamed-of-benefits.

Point is, Carter's making it awfully hard to stick to *my* rule.

Strawberry Tea Committee meetings *should* be keeping me busy. But even so, I've managed to spend way too much time thinking about our beach walk coffee date. And the eager and studious way he watches me when I talk. And the way his arm fits perfectly around me, making all my racing worries not just go still, but disappear.

Anyway. I have *things* to do before he arrives.

"You're the one," I tell the shirt.

Then the doorbell rings.

"Shit! Already?"

I so lost track of the time... and I'm wearing my old jeans with holes in the knees. My T-shirt is splotched from the eight shockingly different white paint samples I tried out in the hallway this morning.

Would he wait long enough for me to change clothes?

Even thinking it makes my throat tighten. No. I'll just embrace the rough-and-tumble look.

I skid to a halt in front of the door, grabbing one of Alph's old baseball caps and jamming it backward on my head.

There. Casual, cool, calm.

"Nnnnnnhohmygod come on, get *open*, door—" I wrestle the damn thing. Shit. Did I lock it? I actually did. The lock won't twist open—oh, wait. Open is the *other* way. "C'mon," I groan to myself. "You *know* how doors work. Even when hot guys are on the other side."

The laughter on the other side tells me that door doesn't block as much sound as I thought. Which is actually useful to know, now that I have a secret to keep within these walls.

"Hot, huh?" Carter greets me when I finally pull the door open. He's grinning like crazy. "Thanks."

He's just standing there wearing a casual, pale grey suit that's been tailored to within an inch of his life. And boy, was it worth whatever he paid. It glides along the planes of his shoulders, skims his chest, sits perfectly on his hips...

I'm willing to bet it shows off his tremendous ass. I almost want to ask him to do a twirl so I can check.

Well, now I feel even more scruffy.

Obviously I wasn't going to shower and change into my

party outfit yet, for filthy-pre-party-sex-related reasons. But I still wanted to change into *nice* clothes.

"Uh, yeah." I shake my head. "Even better without an aging doily between us. Come in."

Carter's lips twitch. "Who's that? Your ex?"

I burst out laughing so hard I almost double over. When I stumble back, he steps inside and takes care of closing the door.

Honestly, Garth would lose his *shit* if he heard anyone call him an aging doily. And I'm not even sure he knows what a doily is.

By the time I catch my breath, Carter's bending over to take off his shoes.

Oh, yeah. I'm going to enjoy the hell out of that ass-tailoring tonight.

"I'll show you what I'm wearing after we have pie," I promise him. "Come on into the kitchen."

"Pie?" Carter stares at me. "It's real?"

"Uh…" I blink at him.

He clears his throat and gestures outside vaguely. "I thought it was an excuse for us to… you know… be alone."

"What am I, a monster? I would never make a sexcuse about a pie," I scoff.

Carter snorts with laughter and shakes his head. "Sexcuse," he echoes me.

I wink at him. "You know, an excuse to—"

"Oh, I know." Carter catches me by the wrist and steps closer, and his scent fills my nose with the mix of cologne and shampoo and all the knee-melting bits that are just *him*…

I'm about to melt into his chest and stretch up for a kiss, but then he holds me at arm's length.

Fuck.

My heart leaps into my throat. Too much? Too romantic? Did I leave the curtain drawn aside on the window?

But no, Carter's reaching into his jacket. And he pulls out...

A red rose. A single stem, stripped of its thorns and wrapped in delicate tissue paper. He offers it to me, and I can't help but notice... his hand is shaking.

I can't quite breathe, either. It's like my body is filling up with static electricity, and the only way to settle the charge is to press myself up against him until I don't know where one of us ends and the other begins.

What's happening?

My jaw hangs open as I stare at the flower.

Carter gulps. "I didn't want to break your rule. Just to say thank you for coming tonight and I'm sorry it's last-minute and I think you're gonna do great, and—"

I gather all my boldness, and then I reach up and press a finger over his lips. "Shhh," I whisper. For just a moment, I want to pretend that I'll let this mean something more.

Every instinct in my body wants to pull toward him. Just as it always has, but a thousand times stronger now that I know what that feels like. Now that I know it makes him happy, too.

I make him happy.

It's almost impossible to believe, and that's what helps me snap out of it.

"Thank you," I add, taking the rose.

I can't help stroking the red petals, nor can I help comparing the smooth glide across my fingertip to Carter's lips.

I mean, if I *did* have a list for what it would take to get me to hand my heart over to someone again, that *would* be on it. But I won't and I don't, and it's out of the question.

"You're welcome," he murmurs hoarsely.

Then there's silence.

We're standing here in the entrance hallway, bathed in late afternoon light, and I'm trying my best not to feel like the foot or so between us is ten thousand miles.

"Come on in. There's pie," I murmur after a few seconds, my brain too blank to remember that we just went over that.

Carter breathes a sigh of relief, and the moment is gone. "I'd love some. Show me a fork and it's all mine."

See? We can be friends. With some pretty enormous benefits, granted. But definitely not the kind of friends who give away their hearts to each other, because that would be a bad idea.

And that's just that.

———

The pie was great. Kissing as we ate the last forkfuls of our pie slices—even better.

But the most delicious part of all is the anticipation as I put the dishes in the dishwasher and turn back to Carter, leaning against the kitchen counter.

"I think it's time to shower and get ready."

Carter looks down at himself, then at me. "I'm ready, aren't I? This isn't too much? Do I need to dress down?"

It's kind of adorable, watching him get so confused. "No," I laugh. It's very sweet that he's suddenly so worried, though. Like he wants to run his outfits past little old *me* for approval.

"I was trying to subtly imply… dessert and a show?"

Before he even turns around fully to look at the TV, I groan with laughter. "Dude! You can watch me shower. All right?"

"*Oh!*" Carter turns bright red and leans on the table to stand up. "That sounds very—I mean, hold on. I'm just getting up. Yes. Yeah, of course. I'd love that show."

"Thought so." I dissolve in giggles, barely propping myself up against the counter as I watch him get all flustered. "I wish I'd known how easy it is to get you all like this, though."

Carter clears his throat and folds his arms. "Only when you surprise me." Before I can argue with him, he freely admits, "That happens a lot."

"Yeah, it does." I bat my lashes at him, raising one foot against the cabinets and swinging my hips from side to side. "I mean, we could always postpone the show until after we get back…"

Carter jerks his head toward the bathroom. "Absolutely not. Get your ass into the shower."

My gasp isn't even pretend. I love how he's suddenly getting all decisive and bossy with me. "Oh! And what if I dawdle?" I tease him.

"Then we have less time for me to do what I want with you."

Okay. That convinced me. I peel myself from the counter and scurry for the bathroom. Carter just manages to slap my ass on the way past, and I gasp as the little burst of heat goes straight to my cock.

I'm almost giddy with delight when I get to the end of the hall and glance back to find him slowly following in my wake. He can't seem to tear his eyes from me. They're dark and intense, hungry in a way that makes me shiver from head to toe.

I feel like a little songbird dancing in front of the jaws of a lion—and all I want to do is preen harder.

"Strip," Carter orders me from behind. I can hardly breathe with anticipation, fumbling with the button on my jeans.

It's perfect timing. By the time he reaches the bathroom and shut the door, I'm waiting for him.

Naked, half-hard, and flushed with the building heat between us.

"Good," Carter murmurs as he looks me up and down. "Very good."

My semi twitches and thickens between my thighs. Being looked at by him—really inspected, from head to toe—it's like nothing else I've ever felt. I shift from foot to foot, biting my lower lip.

"Now what?" I tease him.

"Shower," Carter orders. He settles himself against the kitchen counter, leaning there casually and letting out a sigh.

I hesitate.

Is he okay to stand there for so long? Or is that better than sitting? I'm not really sure, and I don't want to ruin the mood by asking.

Carter's expression softens for a moment. He leans in and down to kiss me softly. Then he repeats, "Shower," in a low growl, and slaps my ass again.

I waste no time getting in the shower. It feels like his gaze is a wildfire sweeping across my skin, making me prickle to life everywhere he looks.

The shower door is clear glass, and the only thing between his gaze and my skin is the thin layer of steam and water droplets that forms on it.

I can't quite make out his expressions, but everything else is fair game... so I assume it's mutual.

It's so strange, trying to shower normally while I know I'm being watched. Not just watched, either. *Wanted.*

It takes all my focus to do everything in the right order, and even then, my dick has a mind of its own. I'm fully hard. It feels impossible, trying to think at all when the stream of shower water makes my stomach go taut with pleasure and my head spin.

Every time I peek at Carter, I find him watching me through the shimmering haze, and I go all tingly again.

"So, how long have you been into me?"

I just gasped at exactly the wrong moment. I think I just filled both lungs with shower water. "Fuck—ow—I mean, what? Into you, as in...?" I cough.

Carter chuckles in a way that tells me he knows that I know exactly what he means. "Sorry. Bad timing."

"Uh, yeah. It was." I don't just mean the shower water. I run my hands over my face, lingering a little longer in the hopes of letting my blush fade away. "Um..."

"That long, huh?" Carter murmurs. He doesn't sound weirded out, though. Or eager. He's just curious, but in this soft, gentle way that makes me feel safe.

So I follow my impulse and admit to it. "A long time. Is that... is that weird?"

"No," Carter says. "It's just..." He pauses for so long I almost think he's forgotten to say the rest of his words out loud, but then they tumble out all at once. "I'm sorry I didn't notice you."

I open my mouth to tell him it's okay, but something just unfurled in my chest—a tighter knot than I ever thought I was carrying with me. So I close my mouth again, reaching for the shampoo to run through my hair. "Thank you," I croak. "I felt pretty weird about it for a long time."

Guilty for lusting after a guy I thought was off-limits. Frustrated for not being able to shake those feelings. But stronger than anything else... that furtive, exhilarating pleasure I didn't even want to try to let go of.

While I'm spilling my heart in the privacy of the steam-covered shower glass, I might as well go all the way.

"I thought I had to try harder to get you to notice me," I admit. "And at the same time, I was afraid of trying too hard and realising you were never really gonna see me that way. So I never really made my mind up."

Carter groans. "Oh, Fox."

Even the nickname makes me pause and smile. It's bittersweet, but it's funny. He *did* notice me—enough to give me a nickname that nobody else had. And I never realized that.

Hell, I'm barely that much younger than him and the rest of the guys. I could have been in the Sunrise Brothers, like Berty thought. If I'd been cool about it.

If I'd been willing to take the risk.

"I promise it had nothing to do with you. When I'm going after something I want, I don't even see anything else," Carter tells me.

It's very sweet of him, but also hilariously unnecessary. I've known all of that since... forever.

"I know. And besides, we were dumb kids. We had to wait til we're older and wiser."

Carter chuckles. "Or at least older. Some of us still attract disaster."

"Hey," I protest, but I can't quite glare at him. Even when I wipe off the mist from the glass, it frosts up again too quickly, blurring all the details from his face. But I can still tell that Carter is watching me intently.

He's not saying anything, either. The more I squint, the

more I think he's got one hand on his own crotch... like he's fondling himself while watching me.

Holy fuck. My dick throbs so *damn* hard.

Huh. Turns out I'm an exhibitionist.

I stop paying attention to washing, and start focusing on touching myself slowly and sensually.

I'm putting on a show.

Water streams down my torso as I run my hands across my chest and down my thighs, reach behind my head and twist around to turn my back to him...

Carter growls softly. "You're clean enough."

I grin to myself, keeping my eyes closed against the water. "I'm not sure I scrubbed behind my ears," I insist, trying to sound innocent.

But I hear his footsteps shuffling closer. "Turn the water off."

I barely hold in the squeak as I do so, and the door yanks open. Carter's standing there holding a towel.

"Step out."

Oh my God, yes. I can barely breathe, I'm so eager for him to finally take over. At last, I'm not the one making up my own fantasies.

They're coming to life and sweeping me off my feet.

"Come," Carter murmurs.

I can't even make the smart-ass joke about not cumming yet. I'm tripping over myself to obey him, to give him everything he wants.

I'll do it all.

Carter wraps the towel around my shoulders as I step out of the shower, my toes curling against the cool floor.

He leans in and presses his mouth on mine until my knees melt under the intense heat. It somehow feels like he's kissing me all over as he drags his lower lip along mine, slips his tongue between my teeth...

Carter abruptly pulls back and steps closer. I step back, so I don't soak his nice suit. He does it again. I'm backing up against something hard—the bathroom counter. There's no further to go.

"Up," Carter growls.

I scramble up, bracing myself with my hands tightly curled around the edge of the counter. Without even being asked to, I spread my legs, unable to help squirming as I stare at the tent in his dress pants.

He's clearly hard as anything. Is he about to fuck me? Right here? I spread my legs a little further, my heart pounding like hell.

But instead, Carter bends over at the waist. He carefully braces himself on his other limbs, resting his forearms on the counter on either side.

Is he about to—holy shit, he already is!

Carter is licking slowly from the base of my shaft all the way to the head.

"Oh, fuck!" I whimper. Sparks burst under my skin, so fiercely that the shower water across my hard-on might as well have been a passing breeze.

This is all wetness, friction, heat... and the sight of Carter bending his head over *me*.

He looks up at me for approval. "Yeah?"

"Yes please yes please yes—"

Carter chuckles, interrupting me by licking my cock again, his nose bumping against me with his eager clumsiness. The wet heat tracing circles, figuring out all the best spots, and the cool air touching the spots he's just licked...

It's heaven. I might as well be flying, and I think I've just invented six new combinations of filthy language.

I grab his forearms, panting for breath by the time he's worked his way around. "Fuuuuck," I choke out.

It ought to be uncomfortable, half-reclining on the cool countertop dripping water everywhere with my head jammed against the mirror... but he's driving me way too wild to think.

"More?" Carter murmurs, like he's savouring his opportunity to tease me. And I immediately regret any teasing I've ever done that might slow down the thing I want—*need*—more than anything in the world.

"Yes, Carter," I gasp. "*Please*. Oh, fuck. Please, please, I need you—" I choke off into a tiny, whimpering gasp.

Carter just closed his lips around my cock, sucking the tip into his mouth. The feeling of tight, wet heat engulfing me makes me throb from head to toe. And it's not over there.

He's bobbing his head now, sucking in a little more each time. He's taking it so slowly that I'm pretty damn sure it's his first time, but he's learning fast.

"Mmm," he groans, the vibration of his throat vibrating through me until I almost plunge over the edge right here and now.

I hiss and fight it back, trying desperately to cling to the edge. I forgot this felt so good. *Has* it ever felt so good? I have no idea. There's no space to think now.

My pleasure is the one thing I'm not used to giving. Or rather, I'm not used to others wanting it. But now Carter does, and he does so with a ferocity that blows my world apart.

If that's what he wants, he can have it. All night long... and then some.

CHAPTER Eighteen
CARTER

Everyone knows the blowjob basics: no teeth, lots of enthusiasm. Coincidentally, that also describes most hockey players I know.

It's my first time sucking another man's cock—or anybody's anything, really. I barely know how to *be* this eager for anyone, but somehow, it comes naturally now.

"Yes! Oh, fuck… fuck, fuck fuck…"

Fox's moans are delicate, and utterly spellbinding. They make me want to overwhelm him with the force of my desire.

He's so sensitive—the slightest of brushes against his skin and he lights up like a Christmas tree. He whimpers without restraint, and he moans my name until it becomes a goddamn symphony.

His cock is velvety, yet firm against my tongue. It almost surprises me how much I love this. Even crouched awkwardly here, looking up at Fox with my mouth full of him makes me almost lose my mind.

"Carter... *yes*," Fox pants for breath. "I'm so close. So fucking—oh, fuck..."

I always thought blowjobs were a one-way street, the other way round. But Fox's pleasure is utterly under my control, there's no doubt about it. I'm almost high with my own pleasure, even though I haven't touched myself since he got out of the shower.

"More," he whimpers. "Just like that, please."

And more is what I give him, because somehow it's not all about me, either. It's really about Fox. All the pleasure I want to give him, the devotion I feel to doing it, and doing it well.

I want to make him feel incredible. And as much as I feel like a clueless rookie, I know I can learn fast. If he gives me a chance... I could spend a lifetime getting better at it.

I suck my cheeks in around him, and he rewards me with the most gorgeous strangled little noise, his fingernails tightening around my forearms.

"Almost... fuck..." He rolls his head back against the mirror, his eyes squeezing closed as he sprawls in front of me.

My poor little Fox. He's clearly so unused to anyone else handling his body, much less his broken heart. And it's not just his body I can figure out how to treat well, given the chance.

But only if he says so... and he won't give me that shot.

I've never felt like this for anyone else. I can't imagine it happening again, at least anytime soon. So I have to drink in everything that I can, *while* I still can.

I suck my cheeks a little tighter, swallow Felix's rock-hard dick a little deeper into my throat, moan a little louder.

He lets go of one of my arms abruptly, tapping at my shoulder. Like I'm not already attuned to the tiniest of changes, much less the tidal wave obviously gathering in his bones.

I want him to fall to pieces in my hands, and in my mouth.

"I—I'm gonna—" Felix's voice cracks. "I'm so—holy fuck! Carterrrr—!"

Fuck.

As Fox plunges over the edge, into the brief and intense world of throbbing, pulsating ecstasy, he leaves me with the best parting gift he ever could: my name, like I've never heard it before.

I've done my job.

And now I don't know what to expect. I mean, the basics are obvious: it's about to get messy in my throat. But will I *like* it?

I'd be lying if I said I've never fantasised about this moment. But reality is here for me. It might just check me right into the boards.

Please let me like it.

Fox shudders against me, and I gulp as the first jet hits the back of my throat. The rest of it follows, coating my tongue, and my head spins.

It's thick, salty, a little bittersweet—and *his*.

I don't just like it. I fucking love it. I want everything of his, all the time, everywhere. Especially when I get to watch him blushing, barely able to peek through his fingers as he watches me learn how to take his load and swallow it like a man.

"Mmph," I announce, pulling my mouth off him with a wet pop to wipe the back of my hand like I just downed a bottle of beer. "Done. That was damn good. Five stars."

At first, Fox giggles in this soft, shy way that completely

charms me. Then the laugh turns louder and helpless as he sprawls back on the counter, his cheeks still pink as he gradually goes soft, and the twitching muscles in his lean body go still.

"What?" Fox whispers, and I blink abruptly.

Shit. I was staring at him, wasn't I?

"Uh. Sorry. You're just..." I trail off, shaking my head. *Hot* isn't quite the word. Obviously he is, but that's not what I mean. *Beautiful* sounds too generic. *Adorable* is true, but not the whole story.

Come on. Think.

Oh, fuck.

Loveable. That's the word I wanted.

Screech. Apply the brakes. Do not pass Go. Do not say it out loud.

I open my mouth and close it again, and then Fox giggles.

"Speechless with how perfect I am?" he teases me, with this little self-deprecating twist to his lips. He even jiggles one foot nervously as he says it, like he's afraid I'll think he believes it.

"Yes, actually," I tell him as I carefully straighten up again. My voice is thick not just with the lingering taste of him in my throat, but the warm feeling that floods my chest. "Close enough, anyway."

God, all I hope is that Fox learns to believe that he's perfect—and he always was. And fuck anyone who ever made him feel otherwise.

My beautiful Fox breathes out a quiet, "Oh," and stares up at me speechlessly.

I want to kiss him. But... it seems kind of rude, considering where my mouth has just been.

So I scan the counter, spot the toothpaste, and grab it to squirt some on my fingertip.

Fox's eyes seem to triple in size. "External use only...!" he blurts out as my finger goes into my mouth to scrub my teeth.

Wait... he thought my finger was going *where?!*

I stop dead, finger still in my mouth, and stare at him. At the exact same moment, he blushes and claps a hand over his mouth.

Then we both burst out laughing, which makes it awfully hard to do the already-difficult job of imitating a toothbrush. By the time I rinse out my mouth, Fox is wriggling down from the counter to stand on his own two feet again.

I sweep my arms around him and pull him into my chest, finally kissing him as deeply and thoroughly as he deserves.

Only when he's moaning and squirming all over again do I finally let him pull away for breath.

"See? There's a method to the madness," I tell him with a smirk.

Fox giggles so hard he snorts. "You could have kissed me anyway. And I have mouthwash. That's probably easier."

"Oh." I blush and look twice, spotting the bottle this time. "Yeah, it would have been."

Felix beams and stands on tiptoe to kiss my cheek, then strolls past me to the bedroom. "What a gentleman."

I follow after him, licking my lips as I adjust myself to try to fit comfortably in my dress pants. "I don't think everyone would agree. Lurking in your bathroom, fully clothed and watching you shower? Dragging you out to sit you down and..."

I trail off, because once again, I'm lost for words.

Suck you off? Blow you? Swallow your load?

Nothing captures the intimacy I felt back there. I could feel Fox giving over to me, handing me the reins so I could make him lose control. The trust he places in me every time I hold him... I never want to take it for granted.

"Take advantage of you," I weakly finish, acutely aware of the throbbing pressure of my cock responding to his words.

Fox smirks at me. There's a look in his eye that makes me catch my breath. "Don't worry. What they don't know is that I can give as good as I get."

He turns and approaches the bed with a hungry little spark in his eye that tells me he has a plan for me.

Whoa.

He has a habit of leaving me dumbstruck, but now more than ever, I'm just staring open-mouthed at him.

Compared to the obedient, shy, sweet Fox I got to manhandle in the shower... this is a whole new side of him. And sure, that Fox is hot enough that watching him blow his load almost blows my mind.

But this Fox? The one who knows what he wants and chases it down? It's something else. Fucking sexy as *hell*. And other words—if I allowed myself to think them, which I won't and I can't.

Because it's starting to hurt, realising that I might not be able to be with *this* Fox for long, as much as I want to.

I can picture it already—being here for and with him, giving him everything I can, watching him grow and grow until he walks into every room in every sphere of life looking like this. Like the Fox he was always meant to be.

God. He's going to be spectacular.

But... we've only got two rules, and this fantasy would break them both. I know that. I do.

Goddamn it. Why can't I just be grateful for everything

Fox is already showing me? Do I always need more-more-*more*?

I only know how to chase what I want and wrestle the most I can out of it. But until now, I've never reached that point, and now I have. Twice, just weeks apart: the potential end of my career, and the furthest this relationship can go.

Fox crawls on all fours up the bed until he's straddling me, still naked and suddenly wreathed in that bossy, flirty aura that makes me so fucking eager to learn anything he wants to teach me.

"Look how hard I got you," Fox smirks, resting one hand on my bulge. I can't help a grunt, pushing up against his palm, but he keeps his touch light. "It would be *mean* to make you go out like this."

My head is spinning. Suddenly I barely even know *what* I want. I have no idea how to do anything yet... but if he wanted to fuck me, I'd let him. In a heartbeat.

I'll let him do anything at all to me.

And that should terrify me, but it doesn't. It just feels like I've been living in the same room all my life and I've stepped out of the front door into the wide open future and pleasures I never even knew I could hope for.

"Lie still," Fox orders me in a whisper, running his palm up and down across the line of my cock in my pants. He braces himself over me, glancing up and down my body—even through my suit—with this half-wild look.

All of a sudden, he's so hungry for me it's like he's been starving for years, and a need awakens in me that I couldn't have imagined before.

Fuck. Please. Touch me, lick me, suck me, grind on me—anything you want.

But Fox doesn't even make me beg. He yanks open the

buttons on my pants and tugs down my underwear, and then my aching cock is finally freed.

"Mmmm," I moan in relief as he runs his palms up and down either side of my cock, firm enough to feel good but not to hurt me.

Never that. I don't think he's capable of it.

"Watch carefully," Fox tells me with a devilish little smirk, and then he closes his lips around my cock and sucks me in—right to the back of his throat.

"Holy fuck…!"

I thought I did pretty well, for a first try. Now I know I've got a *long* way to go… but I'm going to enjoy getting there.

"Fuck, fuck, fuck—" I grab Fox's hair before I know what I'm doing, and his groan sounds… *happy*. I tighten my grip and he nods slightly, like he's encouraging me.

So I keep gripping him tightly as he pulls his head up and swallows me whole again. Heat pulsates through me as he fans the sparks smouldering under my skin into an unbearable flame in the span of a few moments.

I *need* his mouth, and I can't even explain why. I just know that if he pulled away now, I'd fall apart into the tiniest little pieces.

It's not just the wetness and tightness of his mouth, the skill in his lips and tongue, the flicks of his fingertips across my balls and around the base of my shaft from time to time.

It's the fact I can look deep in his eyes and see who's doing it—*truly* see him, know things about him through this silent language that others will go their whole lives never seeing.

There's *so* much more to Felix than meets the eye, and I feel like the luckiest goddamn man alive.

He twists his head back and forth, dragging his lips up my shaft, and then repeats the move.

My whole body tingles and for a second I think I'm gonna cum on the spot. It's so much sensation all at once. All of it good, but *so* much of it. "Fuck. I'm... I'm barely gonna last... if you keep that up..."

My words are falling apart before they can even form sentences, like the tongue dancing along my shaft teased them loose and flung them away.

Instead, I give up on trying to speak. All I do is groan, clutch Fox tightly, and float somewhere way above cloud nine.

I knew I was turned on, of course. But not just *how* turned on I was. I've never been this sensitive before—not even in the longest jerk-off session. And most of them aren't.

My own personal time is usually quick and practical, before bed. Since Fox came back... more extended and several times a day, but still... it's nothing like this.

I barely know where to focus—my nipples pushing against my shirt, or the flushed sweat beading on my forehead, or the way I clench down tightly as he runs a finger along my balls... or the most obvious focal point of all.

Fox's lips dragging slowly along my shaft, and his hazy eyes as he peers up at me.

My hips jerk upward on impulse and I try to settle them back down. The ache isn't too bad at this angle, if I keep my legs how they are... I just don't want to choke him.

Fox chuckles and slides his mouth off me, kissing the tip. "Stop being so polite," he whispers in a gust of warm breath on the rapidly cooling wet skin. It makes goosebumps race across the back of my neck.

"Mmnh?" I grunt, my head spinning. Surely he doesn't mean…?

"Just fuck my mouth."

Oh my God. He *does* mean it.

My jaw drops. But I'm too desperate, too close to the edge to resist taking advantage of whatever he offers me. I cup his cheeks with my hands to hold his head in place, thrusting upward again as carefully as I can while Fox holds perfectly still.

It's mesmerising. I can't stop watching my cock disappearing between those swollen, beautiful lips.

And I definitely can't stop myself from doing it again—and again, faster. But as much as I want to speed up, my breath and my strength are slipping from my grasp in a way I never expected.

Goddamn it. I've been in the best shape of my life for years. *Now* my muscles betray me?

Before the irritation can build up inside my belly, Fox just gently rests his hand on mine and guides it to the back of his head. He pushes down hard on my hand.

"*Fuck*," I groan, and Fox swallows me deeply and stays there with nothing more than a wriggle midair above me. He's waiting there patiently for me to grab his hair, and…

It feels so fucking dirty to *use* him for his mouth. But Fox is getting hard again, squirming eagerly in midair as he glances impatiently up at me.

Fuck it.

My thumbs trace little circles near his ears as I grab his head, his jawline resting in my palms. I push him down to the base of my shaft, crackles of lightning dancing along my skin as he chokes.

"You like that, huh?" I pant for breath. "You want more?"

Instantly, he reaches down to start jerking himself off as he moans and whimpers. He's even trying to nod, like it isn't obvious how much he loves it.

Oh, Fox. I know more than you think.

"I'll give you more," I promise in a growl.

There's no point in being gentle and delicate. Not when both of us need exactly the opposite—right now. So I give in to every filthy fantasy that I just *know* will live rent-free in my brain forever after this, and I show him what I'll do to him as soon as I can.

"I can't wait to *have* you," I growl, watching the flush sweeping over his cheeks. "You'll be the one lying here. I'll be the one on top. But I'm not gonna be using your mouth, Fox."

His whimper is sudden and sharp and *blissful*. He shivers from head to toe, trying to press himself closer to me.

"You're gonna take my cum, and you're gonna beg for more," I promise him.

"Mmmm! Nnh—nngh—mmph—" he whimpers, like he's trying to agree, even beg for more details.

But I'm losing my breath, and my rhythm, and my control. All I can do is slam his head down, burying my cock in his throat over and over. "Yes... yes... fuck," I hiss.

Holy fuck, all my muscles are taut like I'm about to explode. I can barely breathe. I can't stop it now.

I let go of Fox's head, but he keeps his mouth exactly where it is, flattening his tongue under my cock like he's ready for me.

"Fox...!"

It hits like a hurricane, in the best possible way. All I can do is stare through the haze at the one fixed point in my life —the one that never made sense until it did.

Awe. That's what I'm floating away in, once the bliss fades

and I find myself limp from head to toe, breathing raggedly. Just… pure awe.

I never knew it could be like this.

Fox scoots up the bed hurriedly. He straddles me, letting my softening hard-on rest against his ass.

Suddenly I wish I *hadn't* just finished. More than anything, I want to fulfil all the promises I just made. And sure, I'm so sensitive this almost hurts, but I can't pull away from him. I'm too mesmerised.

My wet shaft glides smoothly against his skin, brushing between the curves of his cheeks. Inside, some primal instinct tells me that I already know what to do, and how to do it—how to hold him down and drill him into the mattress.

Holy fuck, I'm getting a second show.

Fox wastes no time jerking off for me. His other hand is on my chest, running across every hard-won plane of muscle as he grins without a hint of shame or shyness.

There he is again—*Fox*. The most Fox that Fox can become. Confident as anything, and completely stunning.

He's also really close to finishing, I can already tell. I tug on his thighs until he finally crawls further up and straddles my chest. Now I can watch the action from a new angle— straight below him.

My dirty talk worked before, so I should say something. Before I can get in my head about *what*, I just let instinct take over. It's done a pretty damn good job so far.

"My sweet little Fox," I growl. "I can't *wait* to fuck you. Having my cock resting on you like that—it's dangerous, that temptation. We'll miss the party."

Fox whimpers, speeding up his pace and swaying above me as his lips part.

I'm in a trance, mesmerised by every little gorgeous detail as I watch him eagerly. "All I want to do is throw you on the mattress. Holds your wrists over your head until you realize you can't tease me anymore. Slide my cock back and forth along your cute little hole. Stretch you open, one finger at a time, and then…"

Fox stares at me, motionless except for the frantic pace of his wrist. *Then what?* I can practically hear him beaming from every fibre of his body.

I can barely hold back my grin. This is going to be incredible. I can already tell.

"Then," I growl, "I'll fuck you *exactly* how you need to be fucked, my little Fox. And not just once. All. Night. Long."

Fox goes tight all at once, throwing his head back as his body forms the perfect arc, frozen in midair for a few precious seconds.

I grab his thighs and tug him forward just in time—and every drop ends up on my face, not my suit.

Huh. It isn't just swallowing I like, either.

I feel like this is bragging, showing off the trophy I've earned from him—and the way Fox stares wordlessly at me makes it even better.

I grin at him. "See something you like?"

Fox doesn't seem to be able to speak yet, but he nods hard.

Both of us are lapsing into silence as we gaze at each other. It feels like we're full of all these words we can't possibly say aloud for fear of shattering this moment.

A hint of Fox's shyness is back, but it's not the same kind as before. Not burdened with self-doubt. Purer, all warm and happy and *glowing* with this joy that makes my very soul light up in a way I haven't felt since…

Not since my last face-off.

Holy shit. I thought there was only one way to find my way back to this feeling. Turns out there's two... and both are equally out of my hands.

Fuck me. What have I done?

CHAPTER
Nineteen

FELIX

My ears fill up with the distinctive buzz as a floatplane makes its final descent. Moments later, the plane lands in the harbour between the mainland and Sunrise Island. All the waiting boats can start to cross again, and the conversations around us at the ferry waiting area can resume.

"Is that our plane? We're not late, are we?"

It'll be late by the time we get back, and the floatplanes stop before dark…

"Yeah, we'll be fine. Don't worry," Carter promises. He makes a little gesture as if to reach for my hand, then hastily lifts his fist to nudge my arm instead. He's a lot gentler than he would be with one of his big, manly hockey bros, so the gesture still seems awkward.

I barely hold in my sigh.

Our life would be way easier if we dropped that whole *don't let anyone know* rule. At least, on Sunrise Island. Our neighbours are going to figure it out sooner or later anyway.

Carter clears his throat. "Yeah. We'll be fine."

There's a few moments of silence while I fidget with the buttons on my shirt and he folds his hands behind his back.

"I can't be out too late," I tell him, even though he already knows. It's just that it'll look weirder if we aren't talking like everyone else here.

But they don't have to hide all the best parts of themselves—the parts they didn't even know about.

"Yeah? Oh, the committee, right?"

"Right," I nod. "Right, yeah. The committee."

"Excited?" Carter smiles at me.

"Um..." I shrug, but he's looking expectantly at me, so I sigh. "Pretty nervous, actually."

He looks confused. "Why?"

I don't blame him. I know all five of committee members. Or rather, they know me... as the little kid in a Jack O'Lantern costume, trailing after his big brother's cool friends. Now I'm going to be telling them how to organize the biggest fundraiser of the year. And that they can't make it a Hawaiian theme this year "just for something different".

Berty's right. I need to figure out a job now that I'm living here, so why not try it? I might even go as far as to say... I think I'd be good at it.

But compared to the pressure Carter faces, it seems stupid to tell him I'm scared of a bunch of nice ladies. At least two of them hand out full-sized chocolate bars at Halloween, for God's sake! Meanwhile his job performance is headline news, and people try to break his bones every day.

Sometimes they even succeed.

"It's nothing," I mumble, scratching my neck.

"Well, look at you two! Going to the opera?"

There aren't enough people waiting for the ferry that

anyone cares about forming a line. So Zach can just wander right up to us and chat, beaming away.

"Recovered from the move yet?" Zach adds before either of us can answer that question, throwing an arm around my shoulder in a casual half-hug before punching Carter's shoulder, dodging Carter's punch back.

I interrupt them by hugging him—and none of this half-hug manly bullshit, a real hug.

Zach laughs. "What's that for?" he tilts his head, smiling despite his confusion.

"Just... thanks. For helping me out on moving day." Oh, shit. I knew four pies wouldn't be enough. I should have made another one for him, shouldn't I? "I've got a pie with your name on it," I tell a little white lie, even if it makes me sweat.

Carter laughs. "Is it the one we ate?"

I blush and clear my throat. "No...?"

Zach grins. "How about you donate the baked good of your choice to the Strawberry Tea for me instead, huh? Save everyone from my baking, avoid the pie ownership dispute... win-win?"

I can't help a laugh. Every islander I've seen since I got the job, I've been soliciting pie donations. Word must be spreading. "Okay, we'll do that. But seriously—thanks."

Zach just punches my shoulder—softly, but somehow completely different from the way Carter did it. "Anytime, man. That's what brothers are for."

Whoa. What?

I glance at Carter, but he doesn't even look like he's humouring me. He just nods and claps Zach's shoulder before they start chatting.

Maybe... maybe Berty's right.

I've spent so long yearning to be part of the Sunrise Brothers, for real. But it turns out everyone—even the guys themselves—already thinks I was. Their awkward shadow, maybe, but still... one of them.

The real problem was that I never let myself believe it.

Ouch.

Carter tells Zach about the party, and the moment he accidentally lets slip it's a fancy yacht party, Zach ribs him for the whole ferry ride.

I smile to myself, but for the most part I try to get used to sitting on the other end with Zach in the middle. Way too far away from Carter for my liking, but this way I won't forget and just reach for his hand, or touch his thigh, or lean into his side, or any one of the hundred things I wish I could do.

But we're about to meet his hockey family. These are the guys he spends every waking minute with. He's letting me as close as he can afford to—and then some. I can't betray his trust by being careless.

I can do this. I have to do this. I can't screw it up now.

Even if I just want to be firmly wedged under his arm in the cool evening breeze off the water.

But we don't get everything we want. I know that now, and my heart's already been broken once from trying to make it happen.

"See you kids later! Don't do anything I wouldn't do!" Zach tells us with a cheerful wave.

Carter chortles, and I don't even have to look at him to know what he's thinking. *There's plenty we're going to do later that I bet Zach wouldn't do.*

After waving goodbye, I shove my hands firmly in my pockets... just in case.

It's just past dinnertime, but on such a warm summertime

evening, most of the waterfront shops are still open. There are couples everywhere I look—the ice cream parlour, the place that makes the cute little special chocolates, the Italian restaurant...

It's hard *not* to notice them.

"Penny for your thoughts?" Carter asks, and I gulp.

"Uh... just thinking we should come here sometime."

Carter lights up and grins as he looks around. "Yeah! Some Sunday morning, we can do the farmer's market, and have lunch, and ice cream..."

"Yeah," I smile, but there's something bittersweet happening in my chest that I don't like paying attention to.

Are we picturing the same thing?

I'm imagining walking around hand-in-hand. Teasing Carter as he horses around with me, until he pulls me in to kiss me deeply.

This one thing that would break both of our stupid fucking rules? I shouldn't want it, but I do. I want it more than anything.

"Here we go," says Carter, pointing at a plane that definitely doesn't have the logo of any of the floatplane companies on it.

Duh. Of course it's a charter.

It looks even tinier than the usual ones, but I swallow back my nerves and smile along through all of it—checking in, Carter chatting to the pilot, the safety talk, and worst of all, climbing from the wharf onto the swaying plane.

"You good?" Carter asks.

"Sure," I tell him. "It's like the worst parts of flying *and* boating put together. I'm great." Then I cast an apologetic look at the pilot, but they both just laugh. Carter winks at me when the pilot climbs in the front seat where he can't see us.

"I fly with this guy whenever I come home for family dinner," Carter tells me cheerfully through our headset, and the pilot gives him a cheerful thumbs-up before he starts doing his stuff.

Before, he means. When he was playing the game. ow, he just has to take a boat across the harbour to his parents' house on the mainland.

I swallow back that feeling again and shake my head.

It's just that he sometimes talks like it's right now, and then I start wondering if he's giving me a glimpse at his everyday life—the one he plans to go back to. And I always knew he would.

But if I'm honest with myself... I know that, despite being glad whenever Garth left me home alone to work late at the office, our relationship would have fallen apart if he'd been on the road all the time.

Okay. The plane is taking off. I can distract myself by looking for my house, and by the time we're in the air, we'll just about be landing.

And then we'll be boarding the yacht, and if Carter's telling the truth about how nice the hockey guys are... it's going to be a good night.

Whatever's churning in my stomach might *feel* like the same thousand miles of red flags I once swallowed back... but this time's different.

It's just nerves, that's all.

It's actually kind of fun, making our way from the floatplane dock to the marina where the yacht is due to leave. It's even more thrilling when I realize the party yacht is on a private slip, and we have to make our way through an iron gate, past two guys in black suits who nod and step aside.

Whoa. I've never been anywhere with private security. I glance back over my shoulder, and Carter claps my shoulder.

"It's fine. Just a precaution," he promises. "The area out there is public, and… you know. Social media."

"Mm," I murmur. I'm too busy clinging onto every little spark of reassurance that his touch provides, wishing I could coax them to stay awake on my skin for longer.

I can already see a handful of people aboard. The boat is fancier than I expected—sleek, black and gleaming—but everyone else is just in collared shirts, some of them even in jeans. So I'm not way underdressed.

And if anything, Carter's just a little bit overdressed. Like he's trying to make a good impression.

"Oh! There's Levine!" Carter grins, raising a hand to wave at the guy waiting outside the boat, chatting to a few others. He speeds up for a moment and then winces, and I clear my throat.

"Not so fast, mister."

He gives me a sheepish grin. "Yeah. I probably should have brought my crutches, huh?"

I stare at him in disbelief. "You have those? Should you—have you been skipping using them?"

Carter gives me a sheepish look. "Around the island, I don't really need to…"

"Uh huh." I raise my eyebrows at him. "We'll talk later."

"Yes, sir," he teases me softly, and then he gives me a warm smile that's meant just for me, and I relax.

It's going to be okay, as long as we're together. The details don't matter that much, do they?

Then we reach the others, and there's cheers and whoops.

I can't help grinning as I stand back and watch them greet each other, slapping each other's chests and backs and gesturing wildly as they talk over each other.

I didn't expect to see such real affection between them. It makes me relax right away, even if they're too busy with Carter to notice me.

I'm used to that feeling anyway. And this is for different reasons.

"Okay, okay, get your ass on board," Levine finally interrupts Carter's summary of his surgeries. "You can tell the story when we're all listening, huh? A lot of the guys want to hear it. Hey! Levine." He turns to me quickly to clasp my forearm and slap my back.

I straighten up to clap his shoulder, but I can sense Carter's gaze on me, so I try really hard not to drop my voice and get all gruff.

He wants me to be myself.

"Hey. Felix," I introduce myself.

"Or Fox, to me," Carter interjects. "But I've known him since we were, what?"

"Too long ago to say," I shake my head.

Levine rubs his hands together. "Welcome, welcome! Come on board, get drunk, share the blackmail material! Drinks on the table!"

I laugh as I cross the gangway into the yacht.

Carter leans in to grin at me. "See?"

"Drinks are on the table next to you," Levine hollers after us, and I glance over to find half a dozen bottles of champagne, and a whole tray of glasses.

"Drink?"

I shake my head. "Not yet. In a bit." I'm nervous as hell, but I want to meet them sober. Then I can prove to myself that he's right, it isn't that scary. "I need to remember names."

He grins at me. "A bunch of us do look alike, but the key is the noses. Count the breaks." My wince makes him crack up.

"Everyone's upstairs," Levine calls out, too. "Stairs on the right. Oh! Hey, Scotty showed! Wrong way, man! The one with the gate and the—no, not that way! Jesus, how does this guy even see a puck coming?"

His voice fades as we climb upstairs, and I find myself grinning back at Carter. "Yeah. Maybe not so bad," I admit.

We turn the corner upstairs into a fancy lounge with soft leather couches lining the walls. There are tables with soft shimmery lighting and appetisers, and that's definitely a full bar with a bartender in the corner. And... a live band?

Whoa. "Just a little party," I grumble.

Carter grins at me. "It is. Relatively. Normally it's Levine's backyard—which is a lot bigger than it sounds."

"Yeah, I'm not going to doubt you there."

He laughs. "But this year there's this guy—he wants to sponsor the team, I think. His buddy had a yacht in the marina. Yadda yadda, you know."

"I'm already here," I tell him, wiping my damp palms on my dress pants. "You don't have to keep selling it." It's cute that he's so worried, though.

"Okay, okay," Carter laughs, holding up his hands as I look around.

The lounge doors are propped open, and a few dozen people are outside. A group of women in cute dresses smile and wave at us, but the guys are clustered around the railing. They're too busy shouting different directions for poor Scotty, laughing their asses off.

Then the crowd parts, and I'm face-to-face with someone I actually know.

Garth.

What the fuck?

No way. He's a stress-induced hallucination or something...

But Carter's looking back and forth between us. It's really him. And now that I'm face-to-face with him, my mouth is hanging open, but I can't find a single word to say.

I didn't expect the fury that rises in my veins until it burns through every inch of me, or the sharp twist in my guts.

What is that? Shame? My cheeks burn with it.

It's not my fault I dated an asshole. It's his fault for being an asshole, I remind myself.

I know that, when I'm on Sunrise Island. But here and now, it suddenly feels hollow. Garth is like this—like an eel. Slippery. The feelings he doesn't want just slide off him and stick to everyone nearby.

Garth looks me up and down—and down again. He stares at my shirt, his eyebrows climbing. Then he looks up and smiles.

My gut twists *hard* with that feeling again, and I might just be sick right now. He thinks I miss him, or at least his apology gifts.

I'd tear my shirt off and throw it in the ocean right now, but I don't want to give him the satisfaction. I want to pretend I don't remember where it came from.

"Well," is all he says, and then he looks at Carter, and back at me.

I've spent my lifetime being aware of how close I am to

the men around me, but I've never been aware of it like I am right now.

I know what else he thinks. And he's right. Fuck.

"Nice shirt. And you are?" Garth says, sticking his hand out right past me and toward Carter to shake.

Carter doesn't take it. My eyes are glued to Garth, but I can feel Carter watching me instead, his brows furrowed. "Felix?"

"Hello," I tell Garth as frostily as I can manage. Then I finally tear my gaze off him, doing my best not to shake from head to toe, and look at Carter. "I think I'll get a drink after all."

CHAPTER

Twenty

CARTER

I might be an idiot sometimes, but I'm not *that* big an idiot.

It takes everything I have to stay calm and not punch first. "Garth, I presume?" I ask the guy, ignoring the hand he's offering me. "Garth Brooks?"

He looks down at it, momentarily offended, but then he smirks and stands *way* taller than he deserves to stand. He's *delighted* that I know him by name. Is it an ego thing?

No. His eyes flicker after Fox's retreating back, and then to me, and I can see the calculations going on in his head.

Maybe I *am* kind of an idiot… but if he thinks that weapon will work, he can think again.

We've been through shit he can't imagine. My teammates have my back, no matter what.

"Carter?" Scotty is finally on board, then, because he comes up behind me and puts a hand on my shoulder, looking bemused.

"Excuse me," I tell Garth, and I catch a flicker of nervousness in his face.

If Garth knows me and Felix are... well, whatever we are... he must have guessed I'm going to tear him a new one.

Good. He can stew in fear for a little while.

Then Garth waves me off with an imperious smirk, and I swear only years of coaching and my busted hip keep me from launching myself at him right then and there.

I storm inside, and Scotty chases me. A few other guys slip after him, surrounding me. Scotty reaches out for my arm, but I shove his hand away.

I don't want anyone's comfort. I want to send *that* asshole a thousand miles away, now. Preferably via cargo ship.

"What the hell, man?" Scotty exclaims.

"I gotta talk to Levine. *Now*."

To his credit, he doesn't even question me. "Okay. He's still on the dock," he answers and follows me downstairs, staying hot on my heels. "Hey! Levine! Get your ass in here."

Levine meets us on the gangway. Whatever he sees on my face, he turns white. "What's wrong?"

"Heads up," I tell him, as cold and furious as I can ever remember being, "I'm gonna throw Garth overboard."

I even turn toward the staircase.

"Whoa, whoa!"

The guys clamour to block my way.

"What—Man, no. The Coast Guard gets called out, and you know that makes headlines, and..." Levine waves toward the photographers.

Shit.

I don't have to recognize his outfit to know it's Fox walking up the slip—not too fast or slow, just like he's part of the scenery. Easy to miss, if you're not me.

"What the hell did he do?" Levine asks. He follows my gaze to Fox, blinks in surprise, and then looks back at me.

God, I want to tell them everything. My buddies would join forces and throw him overboard themselves if they knew a fraction of what I know—which, I'm pretty sure, is only a fraction of the full story.

I shake my head, my lips tight. "I can't say."

"Ah," Scotty murmurs. "Not to you. To…"

"My—" I start, and then I immediately regret the word.

I can't say My Felix now. But I don't want to call him my friend. But he's not my boyfriend, either. I wish he could be. I know they'd be fine with it. It's just…

The gangway shifts under my feet a little as the tide rises and falls. It's appropriate for the moment. My whole world is shifting under my feet, and I barely even know where I stand.

But Felix is walking away.

Some small part of me is whispering, *told you so*. And yeah, I knew I didn't have long with him. I just didn't know *how* not-long.

Why come out now, when it's too late?

My gut squirms. I hate every option presented to me right now—every single one. There's no good way out of this, and I know it's at least half my fault. Probably a lot more than that, if I'm honest.

"Shit," Levine whispers. "I'm sorry, man. Look. We've got fifteen minutes until we leave." He runs his hand through his hair and swaps glances with the other guys. I know he's doing the calculations on how to ask the party host to leave. But it's his frigging boat. "I'll talk to the guys. We can all head back to my place…"

"No." I shake my head and clap his shoulder to let him know none of this is his fault. It's just shit, and sometimes… shit happens. "You enjoy the night. Let me know how it was."

"Carter—" Scotty starts, but the others shush him.

And I walk as fast as I can back up the slip, grateful that Fox is sneaking and not truly running away. Nowhere near as fast or as far as I'm running from my demons, and his are bigger than I'll ever know.

Fuck.

Even here and now, when I have the awful feeling I know what he's about to say... Fox amazes me.

I just wish he could believe it.

CHAPTER
Twenty-One
FELIX

Keep it together, Felix. Come on.

I manage not to run back inside, but only just. Thankfully, the guys coming up the stairs are too busy falling over themselves laughing at Scotty. They barely notice me slipping past them to head down the stairs.

Just around the corner from the gangway are the bathrooms. I turn the corner to the silent corridor, and then I lean against the wall and cover my face with my hands.

Shit.

I shouldn't be here. If I weren't here… nobody ever would have known. Maybe Carter would have wondered about the name and written it off as a coincidence.

I can't do this.

There's a way out. The gangway is right there. Levine and the other guys out there are busy catching up.

They don't notice one little Fox slipping past them, and then I'm on the slip, out in the fresh air but not feeling any more free. I walk slowly to avoid attention, but my face is flushed and my hands are curled into fists.

I'm on the verge of sobbing, or collapsing, or... I don't even know what.

Maybe I should have taken the chance to curse out Garth. But if I did that, he'd just hit back. And it's always, *always* worse.

He'd out me and Carter in a heartbeat. He probably already has.

Fuck Garth!

I growl under my breath, but as much as I hate him, the worst part—the absolute worst part of all—is that I can't blame him for everything.

Those red flags I've been swallowing, so soon after promising myself I'd never do that again... they're mine and Carter's alone. Not Garth's.

He's just a slimy bastard who belongs in this life more than I do, who uses fake smiles and real cash and desperate people to get wherever and whatever he wants. All he did was make me face up to the truth.

I'm not surprised when I hear footsteps behind me, and then Carter's voice. "Fox...? Fox!"

I stop halfway up the slip, hoping we're out of earshot of both the top and the bottom of it. "I can't do this," I whisper aloud, and I'm slowly realising that I don't just mean *tonight*.

And that hits me so hard I swear I can feel it in my stomach. I want to double over, and it takes all my strength not to.

Carter knows, too. He's dead silent.

But it doesn't change the truth.

Fuck.

I can't turn to look at him, or I *will* sob, and then I'm definitely going to attract attention. I wrap one arm around my stomach, but I have the horrible feeling it's not going to settle for a long-ass time.

"I'm sorry, Carter. I can't be what you need me to be."

I can barely hear Carter gulp over the gentle slap of wavelets on the pillars nearby. "I-I'm sorry, too." His voice is hoarse.

I shouldn't run. This party is like a family reunion. I know how much it matters to him that I'm here tonight. But this version of me...? Garth would twist me around his finger before Carter can so much as blink.

And the only thing that would snap me out of it is exactly the thing that's out of bounds.

"I can't do our rules. I never should have in the first place."

Carter lets out a long, weary sigh.

Then, all he says is, "Yeah."

What more *is* there to say? It's just... everything hurts. More than I thought possible.

With Garth, I just remember feeling angry at myself for wasting so much time. And a lot of relief that it was over. This time is so much worse.

Those rules that were supposed to protect us? They failed. My heart is shattering into a thousand pieces, and I don't see any way of stopping it.

CHAPTER
Twenty-Two
CARTER

Fuck.

All I had to do was be a little bit braver, a little bit faster.

I could offer everything in the world now. I could offer to tell my buddies everything, have him on my arm all night, kiss him in front of all the press that are, predictably enough, gathered right outside that iron gate.

But it's too late.

I swallow hard as Fox looks up at them and freezes. "Shit."

I have to help him with this. Everything else comes later.

"We'll take the plane home."

Felix glares stubbornly at me. "I can…" he trails off, and I wait. "…take the ferry," he finally finishes in a mumble.

We both know the terminal is nowhere near downtown Vancouver, and it would take hours. A private chartered plane? Twenty minutes.

"Please," I tell him softly. "It's the least I can do."

Felix looks at me, and he quickly looks away again. I can

see the gathered tears in his eyes, and it's like a vice grip squeezing around my heart.

I caused that pain.

And I can never, ever forget that.

"Okay," Felix finally whispers. "Just... get us through your—that—mob."

I flinch, recoiling from his words. He's being incredible right now. I can sense how hard he's holding onto all these painful bits of himself, trying to avoid causing a scene.

All for my sake.

But it's not *my* mob. Or a mob at all. They're just people who are excited to see the whole damn team get on a yacht.

And that little voice is back—the doubting one, the one that told me I wouldn't be able to get a real job playing hockey, and then told me once I did that it would all be over soon. And it turned out to be right.

This is why we don't work together.

Fuck. I thought me and Fox fit together so perfectly. Even on board, he just had to smile and say nothing and *know* that I care more about him than anything—anything at all—Garth could say or do.

But the moment he saw that asshole, the confident new Fox I've been falling for just vanished. And then everything went wrong.

The rules were always the problem. He's right. I just wish... it didn't mean that this was over.

"Let's get out of here," I murmur, trying to keep my voice from croaking too badly. It's stabbing through me like a knife, that newest and worst reason I can't take his hand. "Follow my lead."

And Fox does.

He always does, whether or not I deserve it.

But that crowd—that, right there, is the reason for my rule. And Felix's rule? I suddenly understand it. I *get* why he'd want to avoid this, even if I'm not sure it ever worked.

I thought I understood the worst kind of agony when they carried me off the ice, delirious with pain and knowing full well that this would probably be the end.

Turns out, that was just practice. This is the real game. I've lost, because let's face it: I took my shot too soon and clumsily. I've learned that lesson in the game over and over, yet I still didn't learn it well enough.

I held back when I should have given it my all... and now time has run out.

CHAPTER Twenty-Three
ALPH

It's hard to surprise people on Sunrise Island.

Especially when you show up at the ferry and the skipper welcomes you aboard, does a double-take, and then tells you, "Hey, do you know you just missed Felix and Carter? I think they were going to some… party?"

Only then did I remember Flick saying something about a party. This last week, it's all been a blur of rushed packing, so I could drive out here early and surprise him.

Fair enough. Surprise guests get surprised.

I didn't see much point in hanging around on the mainland when the moving truck is all locked up at Murph's boatyard overnight. So I headed over to the island anyway, and immediately got cornered by Berty to hear everything about my little brother's new position as the Strawberry Tea planner.

Sounds like hell to me, but it's up Flick's alley. It's exactly what he needs to mend his broken heart and get over that asshole. And even better, Carter will be the guest of honour.

I'm glad Flick has someone he can really count on.

The only problem is that I showed up here, at my old-yet-new home, and found the door *locked*.

What the hell? Has there been a crime spree here?

At first, I decided to sit outside and wait instead of breaking a window, but I gotta say, a little breaking and entering is becoming steadily more attractive. I could just climb up the maple tree and into my old bedroom window, but I'm a foot taller than I was when I last tried it.

And would you look at that? The window's left open a crack! If I don't break my neck, I've got a pretty good chance of getting inside...

Wait.

I hear crunching gravel. I'd tune it out as just another passing golf cart, but it's slowing down and stopping, and I hear voices.

Aha!

"We don't need any more adventures, you and me," I tell the old tree, patting its trunk with relief before I head around front.

By the time I get there, the golf cart's gone. But Flick's walking up the front path—and his head is hanging.

Fuck.

I stop in my tracks in the side yard, just staring at him for a few seconds. And more than ever, I want to find Garth and give him a swift kick where the sun don't shine.

Then I start moving, and Flick sees me. He claps a hand over his shriek just in time to muffle it, but he almost jumps a foot in the air.

"Whoa! It's just me!" I raise my hands. "Surprise!"

"Surprise—you can say that—what are you—what the hell?" Flick's voice slowly climbs back down to its normal levels by the time I reach him and clap him on the shoulder.

"Get ready!"

"Oh, God, not tonight—"

"Big brother privileges!" I pick him up for a hug and spin him around just like I used to—exactly like he hates.

Flick groans and smacks my chest when I put him down, but at least he's managed a glimmer of a smile.

I was trying to play it cool, but... honestly, he looks *awful* up close.

"Shit. Are you okay?" I ask him, scratching the back of my neck as I study him.

Flick averts his gaze. "I'm fine," he lies, as terribly as always. "Seriously, though. What *are* you doing here, Alph? Besides scaring the shit out of me."

"You locked the door!" I protest.

Flick scoffs. "Of course I did. There could be... werewolves."

"On Sunrise Island."

"Yes. Anyway, I mean, what are you doing here *now*, not next week?" Flick smiles again at me, like he's happy to see me, but good God. The more he tries to put on a show, the more worried I'm getting about him.

I don't want to tell him I dropped everything and rushed here so he wouldn't be alone. But that's exactly what I did when Drew told me about the shoeboxes. I knew it must have gotten worse, but not... *this* much worse.

What a fucking prick.

"I finished up early, thought I'd surprise you," I tell him with a grin. "Got any beer?"

Instead of inviting me in to hang out and drown his sorrows, Flick just shakes his head. "I think I have half a bottle of wine. You can finish it, if you want," he offers. "I'll bring it around back."

That doesn't sound like sharing it and spilling our guts and brotherly bonding time to me.

"Nah, it's fine," I wave off the offer instead. "Not inside? The easy way?"

He furrows his brow. "I don't know. I just thought… privacy…?" he trails off, and something seems to be making him even more upset all of a sudden. He heads up to the porch and climbs the stairs, fumbling for his keys.

Shit. "Oh, yeah. Of course. It's not like we're having sleep-overs," I laugh, following after him.

Flick opens the door and steps inside, then passes me the downstairs keys in a way that means he's not letting me in. I raise an eyebrow and he shakes his head. "Just tired," he lies again, equally terribly. "I gotta get my sleep."

"For the Strawberry Tea committee! I heard all about it —*alllll* about it—from Berty. Good job, little bro."

"Thank you," Flick mumbles, leaning on the edge of the door.

I can usually get a groan out of him, if not a laugh, so it's worth a shot. "Now, there's a phrase not to mix up. Or Strawberry Terry Committee. Or Strawberry Titty—"

"Good night, Alph," Felix groans.

I wouldn't normally push him this much, but now I'm getting really worried. I put a hand on the door. "No, really, though. Flick. You sure you're good? You look, uh…" I trail off, clicking my tongue and grimacing.

Huh. Wait. I'm just noticing how nicely he's dressed up. And someone dropped him off.

My heart skips a beat.

"Bad date?" I guess.

I'm hoping I'm wrong, but Felix just flinched. Shit. I'm close.

"*No,*" Felix scoffs. "I'm not dating anyone. That would be dumb. In fact," he folds his arms, "I've decided not to give my heart away to anyone who doesn't deserve it. Because I'm sensible now. And… you know. Self-respecting."

"Riiight," I nod slowly. That tone makes it sound like he *resents* respecting himself.

What am I not seeing?

"I'll let you get some sleep, and we can talk in the morning, huh?" I suggest.

Flick rolls his eyes. "What a great, and also original, idea."

The sarcasm is impossible to miss, and I can't help but laugh.

"Yeah. You should have told me you were tired and you wanted to go to bed," I smirk at him, raising my hand to wave. "Good night, Flick. Catch you in the morning, if you don't run fast enough."

He rolls his eyes, but he can't hide the glimmer of a smile. I feel a little better as I head around the back. At least I'm here now, and I can start doing my job as a big brother.

But there's something I'm not seeing.

Felix's heart is broken. Definitely. It makes me ache to see him looking so lost, so adrift in a way that isn't usually like him at all. But this seems different, somehow, from the angry, upset Flick I talked to on the phone after the breakup.

Whatever happened, it's big, and it must be out of left field.

As I unlock the door and flick on the lights, I try to figure out what the craziest thing I could think of would be. The truth must be somewhere between my guess and that, whatever it is.

I mean, the *craziest* thing would be if Flick and Carter…

Oh. *Oh.* No way.

I stop dead in my tracks, right in the doorway.

"He didn't," I whisper aloud, like that will make it true. "They wouldn't. It doesn't make sense, except... it does."

Flick's into guys.

I thought Carter was straight—he's never corrected anyone about it. But then he's never mentioned anyone. Not a name, not a gender, not a fleeting mention of a single person.

And it goes way beyond gender. I know them both.

Flick puts himself second any day of the week, if someone will tell him that he belongs.

And without the game, this one thing that's driven him for his whole life, Carter will be lost. Looking for another team to play for, so to speak. People get drawn to him—it's why he got support behind the scenes so quickly, and a fan base of his own even quicker. He was on track to be team captain.

Carter is exactly the kind of beacon that a delicate moth like my little brother would be drawn to in the longest nights of his life.

It makes a horrible, *horrible* kind of sense.

Oh, Jesus.

So I don't think twice about it. I pull out my phone and I text the group chat a few times in quick succession.

Guess who's here???? Who wants a beer?

and can bring the beer

and can host bc Flick's sleeping

Zach and Drew type right away.

Fuck YES! says Zach.

Drew is even more enthusiastic. *THE BOYS ARE BACK!!!!!*

Murph sends a thumbs up and a beer emoji, which is about right for him.

That just leaves Carter. He's online. He's seen the message, but he's not saying anything.

Carter? I ask.

He types, stops.

Types again.

Stops again.

Shit.

My suspicions are growing by the second. I stare at my phone, my grip tightening just like my jaw.

He doesn't want to face me.

Well, he's gonna have to deal with it, because I have something to say to him.

Drew spams the chat, oblivious to the vibe in here.

DUH! Sunrise Brothers Cove!!!

We meet as the sun sets, my brothers

Actually that just sounds cool and I don't know when sunset is, we meet right now!!!

Last one there buys the next case

GO WELL AND FAST, BROTHERS

It would be funny if I weren't still waiting on Carter to say anything at all.

Zach thumbs-up Drew's last message, and then Murph does the same. I follow suit before going back to staring at the screen.

After what feels like an eternity, the little *3* next to the thumbs up emoji turns to a *4*.

Good.

CHAPTER
Twenty-Four
CARTER

Late-night beers on the beach. Just like old times.

It should feel good. If I can't be with my team, I can be with my brothers. I should be happy. Like Drew said, everyone's back together again. A day or two ago, I would have been thrilled. I'd have run there, busted hip or not.

I'm gonna be the last one there, so I take my time changing out of my date—*party* outfit—and into jeans and a T-shirt.

Those long summer days mean it's not quite dark yet. Even so, I move to the side of the gravel road when I hear a golf cart on the road.

"Need a ride?"

Wait… that's Drew. I thought he was racing to the beach. But I guess he was rushing so he could pick me up.

That's… God, that's stupidly considerate of him.

"I guess I won't say no," I bluff, and he lets me keep my pride.

"Hop on in."

When I turn, I find a much nastier surprise: he's not in his own golf cart.

It's...

"Frog," I almost croak.

Drew winks at me. "Like new!" He grins like he expects me to be relieved. And the new bodywork does look great, I have to admit. He just has no way of knowing how goddamn painful this is.

When I manage to unfreeze, I clear my throat. "Yeah, just—wow. Surprised," I manage.

"I thought I'd leave him overnight somewhere. See if he's still running in the morning." He winks at me. "If I'm lucky, someone will run into him."

I elbow him, but before he can take off again, I hear another voice.

"Room for one more?"

Shit.

It's Alph.

I plaster a grin on my face as he hops up and hugs us both, but I'm sure I'm not imagining the look he gives me first.

Shit. There was just something about the way he suddenly suggested drinks, and he said my name in the chat and everything...

As we get rolling, I can't quite look at him. Or Frog. Or Drew. Which means I'm pretty much focused on staying in a comfortable sitting position, which is tough on a bouncy road and an uncomfortable seat.

I've walked *way* too much tonight. My surgeons are gonna kill me.

To be honest, the pain is kind of a relief, though. It sort of helps me tune out Drew describing all the bodywork repairs in great detail, because I can't work out how to tell him to quit it without letting him in on the not-very-secret secret, too.

"Wait," Drew stops himself after a minute and looks at Alph. "Have you heard yet? Oh, man."

"Heard what?" Alph asks, but he's looking straight at me. His gaze is boring into the side of my head, in fact.

I don't think this is gonna be good.

"That story can wait," I tell Drew too firmly for him to argue, and thankfully, it isn't much longer before we're there.

It takes me a little while to get down from the seat, but Alph waits for me, which doesn't exactly help the growing feeling of dread gnawing in the pit of my stomach.

Not now, man. Any other time but now.

Drew goes ahead, and Alph silently walks alongside me, all the way through the woods and down to the beach.

Just before we get to the cove, Alph stops me.

"I know," he tells me quietly.

I mean, that was obvious. But hearing it out loud—seeing him watch me like he's levelling an accusation at me that he expects me to deny, like I'm ashamed of it...

I look down.

Fuck.

Why does this fear have to come true after it's already too late for it to matter?

"How could you? *Why* did you?"

Here we go. I've been waiting for Alph to blow. He cares about Fox—a lot. Finding out your best friend is with your little brother... or *was* with... actually, I don't know what he knows. That's gonna make this tough.

"Hold on," Zach interrupts us. "What—"

"Stay out of it," Alph tells him.

The others abruptly go quiet and start watching us.

"Flick's been made homeless, unemployed—not like that asshole ever frigging paid him for everything he did—and dumped all at once," Alph tells me with a quiet fury he's never aimed at me before. "That's rock bottom."

I can't disagree, so I grunt and nod.

"So... why *now*?" He points at me. "You know he always looked up to you. Hell, idolised you. And I don't know what happened—and I don't want to know, but I have a pretty good guess."

Heat creeps along my cheeks.

The best time of my life, however brief it was.

I won't deny it, but the less said about that... the better for everyone.

"Yeah," Alph snaps and gets in my face. "Yeah. I thought so. Just because hockey went and left this hole in your life, you wanted to try to fill it with—him?"

Zach starts to move toward us, but Drew puts a hand on his shoulder. Murph folds his arms and watches us as closely as a tennis match.

"You couldn't go fuck one of the *million* guys out there who *can* fool around and keep their hearts out of it?" Alph jabs me in the chest with a finger. "It had to be *Flick*?"

I draw my breath, but I don't have the words. Whatever happened, I can't even explain it to myself. What can I possibly say to him?

Whatever this was, it just... *happened*.

Did I fuck Fox? I don't know what counts, in gay world. But it doesn't matter anyway. The sentiment's still true.

All I know is it feels like there's a void in my life where Fox used to be. And maybe he's right. Maybe it was the same void that hockey left, and I *was* trying to fill it however I could.

Now I've lost both, and I don't know what I'm going to do.

"He *idolises* you," Alph says again, his voice tight with pain. "Are you even gonna stay here? Or are you running back to the ice the moment the doctors clear you? Leaving me to pick up the pieces of his heart *again*?"

I look up at him and raise my shoulders helplessly. Yet again, everything he's saying is fair... and I don't know.

"You don't have *anything*?"

Then Alph shoves me in the chest. I've been expecting it, but without crutches, I can't exactly brace for this. I wince and crumple, grabbing my hip and catching my weight on the other leg. By the time I straighten up, Drew's helping me get my balance. Zach got between us at lightning speed, and Murph is steering Alph away.

But everyone keeps waiting for me to talk.

"Look."

But I *still* don't know what to say, and now my whole goddamn world feels like it's crumbling around me.

I sag against Drew, a lot more than I meant to.

"Whoa. Come on, buddy," Drew tells me, steering me to the cove. The other guys shift around and make room, sit me down and put a beer in my hand.

Even Alph is holding back, giving me time now that he's got his rant out.

I sigh, gripping my beer bottle tight as I try to figure out where to start, but... how can I possibly explain to anyone who isn't Fox?

Murph's the first one to talk. "What didn't you tell us before?"

Fuck.

I know *that* answer, and it's gonna feel like tearing my heart right out of my chest again. I swig my beer to wet my mouth, gulp hard, and try it anyway. Short and to the point.

"I love him."

Even to my own ear, my voice sounds... pretty goddamn awful.

Alph's anger fizzles away, almost as fast as that. He slowly sits down next to me and watches me really close for a minute. Then he grabs a beer of his own and leans against the curved slope of the cove, thumping his head against it.

"Well, shit," Alph concludes.

"Yeah." My voice cracks, so I clear my throat and drink deep.

Alph puts a hand on my shoulder, and I cover it with my own to accept his apology, shaking my head.

I don't blame him for a second. Fox *is* that perfect—that deserving of protection, and of someone getting so mad about him, and someone who looks out for his best interests above all.

Alph sighs and slowly lets go of me, nodding to himself again as he drinks.

"Is it... definitely over?" Zach asks cautiously.

Everyone pauses and looks at me—even Alph, the bottle still tipped at a risky angle.

I press my lips together hard, because that's another answer I think I should know, but I wish to God I didn't have to say it out loud.

But they're still my brothers, because they don't make me. Instead, they just grunt, nod to themselves, and settle down on the rocks around us, and I let the question slip away without comment.

Murph sits with his back to the tide, Drew on the lowest rock at the mouth of the cove. Zach squeezes in beside me and Alph.

"Worried we'll start hitting each other again?" Alph cracks a half-joke.

"That would imply it was a fair fight," Zach says, side-eyeing him, and Alph is gracious enough to duck his head and take the comment.

I think Fox was right, earlier. Maybe we were just doomed from the start.

I need someone who'll let me unapologetically love him, not just fuck him. And Fox needs a man who's brave enough to tell the world that Fox is *his*.

Oh, fuck. I don't know which thought hurts worse—the idea that someone else will find him and love him the way he deserves, or the idea that they won't.

My poor Fox.

Ugh. No. Not *my*, and not *Fox* to anyone but me. And he's a thousand times stronger than he'll ever let himself believe —too strong to need anyone's pity—so not even *poor*.

That doesn't stop me hurting enough for both of us.

"You guys didn't know, either, did you?" Alph asks, and I don't have to look up to see them shake their heads.

I sigh, flipping over rocks like I'm hoping to find the answer to everything underneath one of them. "It's not you, it's me. Ha. But really."

"Sometimes," Alph says with a reassuring fondness, accompanied by a sigh, "sometimes, you can be a real idiot, Cart."

Even I manage to laugh. It might hurt, but it's true. "Yeah. I guess I'm getting what I deserved," I shrug as I finally look up at him.

The serious look on Alph's face stops me. "No. This isn't what either of you deserve, and you know it. This is *love*, man. You really gonna give up that fast on my little brother?"

"Dude. You were about ready to punch me out for *loving* him, like, thirty seconds ago," I gesture with my beer bottle, and everyone laughs.

Alph shrugs and smirks at me. "Changed my mind."

I grunt and flip him off, but the tension easing makes me breathe a little better. Despite his joke, we all know what really changed. My best friends are seeing something in me they've never seen before.

It might have been a while, but these guys still know me better than almost anyone. And I trust their judgment.

Alph jabs me in the ribs. "So?"

"Ow," I complain and look at Zach, who holds up his hands.

"I'm not the referee. I'm just here to stop you two killing each other. Heavy bruises are cool with me."

"Kinky," Murph chooses that moment to comment, making us all laugh for real.

Now it feels a little more like we used to.

When I catch my breath again, I shake my head. "No," I answer Alph's question about giving up on him. "Of course I don't want to. But… it's the decent thing to do, right?"

Alph looks at me thoughtfully, tapping his bottle against his knee. "How'd you know you love him?"

I shrug helplessly. I could describe the way Fox smiles and my heart skips a beat, or the way my world seems brighter when he's in the room, or the way I want us to entwine so tightly that we can't tell ourselves apart, but we're growing *together* into a future that's ours, and ours alone…

But all of it is just dancing around the edges of something else—a knowledge that lives in every cell of my body.

"I just know."

Alph nods like he isn't surprised. "So... fuck the decent thing to do. Or the easy thing. And fuck everyone else, even me." He holds up a hand as Zach opens his mouth to seize the easy joke. "You, shut up."

Zach rolls his eyes but keeps his mouth shut anyway.

"That voice inside you. The one that just knows," Alph goes on. He's looking out at the ocean, but he's still talking to me. "Listen to that. It'll know what the *right* thing is."

It sure feels like that voice has led me straight from the frying pan into the fire, so I'm not sure I believe him.

But I sure hope he's right.

CHAPTER
Twenty-Five
FELIX

Why does self-respect have to hurt so much, anyway?

Let's not kid anyone. This is the source of a lot of the rest of it. So having this blow up in my face was always going to hurt, even if I succeeded at keeping my heart my own. Which I obviously didn't, because I can feel my heart aching with every goddamn beat.

At least, despite Alph's threats, he didn't even interrogate me the morning after he arrived. It was sweet of him to worry, but keeping this a secret is already driving me crazy.

It feels like the worst possible time for all of this to happen—especially when my star guest is no longer *my* star guest—but there are a hundred decisions to make and details to iron out, all of which keep me distracted.

At least I'm not moping all over the island. In fact, I've thrown myself into it so much that I could walk into this final committee meeting with my head held high, and tell them completely sincerely that we're ready for anything to happen.

We'll have enough food, not too much tea, and *one* design

scheme. The extra ferry crossings are triple-checked, posters printed and distributed, the press alerted, you name it.

Most importantly, we've still got our star guest lined up. I mean, I haven't personally checked. I should have, I know. And I was ready to be a professional and text Carter. But Alph unknowingly saved me midweek, when he mentioned that Carter was getting his suit dry-cleaned for the occasion.

I think I managed not to whimper or anything, either, which I can honestly be proud of.

"Unless there's anything else?"

Oh, shit. Marianne spoke loudly and slowly enough that I'm pretty sure it's not the first time she's said it.

"Um, sorry. I was—I was elsewhere," I laugh sheepishly, staring down at my notepad.

My doodles in the margins all look like little waves, and upon them, a little triangular boat.

Fuck.

I flip my notebook shut. "Uh, nothing more from my end," I tell them, and I focus on packing away my planner and pencil case and everything into my bag as they do all the official meeting adjournment stuff.

Before I can stand up, though, Marianne stops me. "Felix. We can't thank you enough for everything you've done this week."

"Oh, thank me after it all goes smoothly," I smile. "Or not. We'll see, won't we?"

She smiles, but she reaches across the table to touch my hand. "Is everything all right?"

Goddamn it. Maybe I *am* moping all over the island.

"It's..." I trail off, and then I clear my throat. "I'll feel better after tomorrow."

"When you see that all the cakes and pies and pastries *did* turn up?" she asks with a glint in her eye. "Or after we know how much we raised?" Before I can answer, she casually adds, "Or when Carter does turn up like he promised?"

"You're just cataloguing my nightmares now. Get out of my bedroom." The ladies all chortle as I groan and stand up. "But... all of the above, really."

Marianne nods. "You've done your best, Felix. You really did. What happens now... happens."

My mouth suddenly feels dry. I swallow a couple of times before I manage to smile. I have no idea what I'm saying to extract myself from the situation, but somehow autopilot is saving me.

As I walk home and rummage in my bag to check that I have *every* notebook, pad, and planner I brought, I find something else I didn't put in there.

It's a chocolate bar. And with it, a greeting card with a little painting of a field of lambs leaping through a field, which confirms my suspicions—exactly the kind of thing Marianne would pick. On the front, it says *Welcome Home.*

There isn't a message inside aside from the signature of all five committee members, but that's not the part that matters. It's the chocolate bar—full-sized, of course. And, more than I want to admit, the front of the card.

After what Marianne said, I have the feeling it's not *just* a welcome home card, either.

"Hm," I murmur to myself and pop them both back in the bag, shouldering it again to keep on walking home.

Garth picked all the art in the old place, of course, and my new home needs artwork of my own. Maybe I'll get a frame.

If all goes well tomorrow, I'll take myself to town on Sunday morning, go to the farmer's market... treat myself to ice cream. Maybe cry a bit... just to celebrate.

Okay, fine, I'm scheduling time to cry into my ice cream. And I'm going to goddamn look forward to it. Because next week, without this whirlwind event to plan for and pull off…

It's not just the time stretching out ahead of me that feels empty. It's… it's *me*.

But I'll never admit it out loud.

CHAPTER
Twenty-Six
FELIX

Just as Marianne predicted, it looks like this year's Strawberry Tea is going to be just fine.

Okay, that's understating it a little. We have a lot of strawberry baked goods, and a *lot* of people here to eat them —more than I can ever remember seeing.

There's only one little problem: I know how many of them are mainly here to see our guest star, their hometown hero, and everyone's heartthrob.

Carter Haywood.

For a good cause, I remind myself over and over. *Plus, the beginning of my portfolio. More people turning up isn't a bad thing. The timing is just another little joke from the universe.*

I've been through worse. I can grit my teeth, ignore my aching heart, and keep myself busy cutting pies and curating the music.

It's obvious that several journalists have turned up just for him, but that's not stopping me. With all the excited charm I can muster up, I'm pressuring them into taking notes and even photos of the event itself—the thing they're supposed to be covering.

Turns out I'm pretty good at it. Some of them even look like they're enjoying themselves now, even though everybody is still keeping an eye out for Carter.

He's fashionably late, which isn't like him. Just late enough that I'm starting to worry, in fact, as I do one more round of the community centre's playing field-sized lawn, casually looking around in case everyone here somehow missed him.

That's when I hear it—the distinctive *purr* of a car engine.

I stop dead, clipboard in hand, and turn toward the road, and the little parking area full of golf carts.

It's impossible to miss the arrival of one bright red VW Beetle—and stepping out of Ladybird, the one man they're here to see. The same one I've managed to avoid seeing all week, but haven't managed to avoid thinking about for longer than a minute.

Fuck.

Carter's wearing that suit again—the grey one, this time with a cream linen shirt and those dumb aviator sunglasses that make him look so stupidly hot. He steps out of the car and closes the door, looking every inch like a movie star who just airdropped in from Hollywood.

Fuck fuck fuck I want to swoon and cry at the same time.

This *really* isn't fair.

I swallow hard, but before I can even turn to find him, Berty's voice comes over the sound system to introduce our guest star.

He's handling all the MC stuff. It's my job to make sure everyone ends up where they should be, and with exactly what they need. And between all the autographs and photos and Carter flashing his grin to the crowd and shaking hands, I can just about lose myself in the whirlwind.

Until we get to the crowning jewel of the day—a huge, fluffy yellow cake with strawberries dotting every inch of it, icing sugar dusted across, and layers of cream sandwiched in the middle.

Carter tucks his sunglasses into the V of his shirt so he can pose with Berty behind the cake. Then Carter turns to look for the knife, and of course, I'm there to do my job. I'm holding the knife with the handle towards him, blade tucked safely into my hand.

We freeze. Hell, time itself seems to freeze. I don't think I can even unwrap my fingers from around the handle.

Fuck.

I stare up into his eyes, and all I can remember is the taste of his lips and the warmth of his skin. I miss him so bad I just...

I can't express it. All I can do is look in his eyes and stop dead in my tracks.

Beneath all this cool and charm and calm, I can sense a thousand layers that nobody else here can.

All of it: his irritation at the photo flashes, halfhearted amusement at his own participation in this whole circus, eagerness to help out, for a good cause...

And a breathtaking pain that flashes through his eyes, the same as mine.

Then, Carter reaches out again. He takes the handle with one hand, but his other rests gently under mine, like he's coaxing me to let go.

I don't think it's static electricity crackling through us, but hell, it might as well be.

My lips part as I stare up at him, heart suddenly

hammering at my ribs.

As soon as I let go, he'll be pointing the knife tip right at my ribs.

But literally, this time.

The corner of Carter's lip lifts up in a little smile—sad and knowing—and suddenly, like that, my breath whooshes out, and I can uncurl my aching fingers.

Just because he saw me.

My head is spinning. I barely know what's happening—Berty's steering us through it all, putting his hands on our shoulders and chatting with the camera guys and posing for ridiculous photos, arms outstretched behind the cake to show how huge it is.

I could just about kiss him, if I weren't so very, *very* focused on kissing one man in particular—the one now holding a cake-covered knife.

He looks down at it and creases his forehead thoughtfully.

Panic seizes me. "Absolutely do not lick the knife," I order him, lurching forward. Carter just grins sheepishly and gives up the knife before raising his hands.

"Guilty," he confesses. For a second, we share a smile, and it's like nothing happened.

Then something flashes over Carter's face, and he looks at Berty. He reaches out for the microphone, and Berty hands it over.

"Folks—all of you islanders, mainlanders—that means you guys from Vancouver Island," he teases them as people chuckle, "and I hear there's even some *main*-mainlanders from further afield?" Carter waves to them when they cheer. "All of you, thank you for coming out today. This fundraiser means a lot to me. This is the fundraiser that... well," he scratches his neck and shrugs. "If it hadn't been for the inaugural Strawberry Tea, I wouldn't have had somewhere to live." He grins. "The hockey court, dawn to dusk, every day of the summer."

The crowd laughs, and so do I.

It's mesmerising, watching the way he speaks so effortlessly. It's obvious that he knows how much he shines, yet he's never lost touch with where he came from. Literally, because we're standing here. But I mean that humbleness too, and his wry humour about himself.

Fuck. He had my heart before either of us even knew about it.

Despite it all, when I stand next to him, every strawberry in eyeshot—and believe me, that's a lot of strawberries—every damn shade of red looks a little bit brighter.

He turns to me the moment he hears my laugh.

"And this year, a little birdie tells me it's our best ever. So, from the bottom of my heart, thank you."

It's a pretty good round of applause, but he's not done.

"And now, there's one man who turned this fundraiser from a..." He coughs and mumbles into the microphone, and people laugh again, "...into a success. Not many people could do that. And I can honestly say, I haven't met many people like him, either. Let's give a huge round of applause to the man who made this happen—Felix Harris."

My ears ring and my head spins, and I'm pretty sure I'm just a smiling statue until—thank God—the applause ends and Carter starts talking again, so people look back at him.

Okay. Conclusions so far: I still love him, and I'm also going to kill him.

"And one more little thing, if you'll humour me," Carter adds, and Berty grins and spreads his hands. "My publicist is gonna kill me for this."

That gets everyone's attention.

Even mine.

Carter shifts on his feet, moves back a little, so he can look *sort of* at the audience, but really just at me for a second before he talks.

"But I want folks here—no, I want one person in particular here—to know this first of all. I'm sorry I was a little late. I was in Vancouver, giving them my decision on my future as a player."

You could hear a pin drop all of a sudden. And I can't breathe.

"I've spent my whole life until now working to get to this point, and… I'm so grateful I got this far. I have a long, long list of people to thank along the way. But I'm also grateful for everything that's happened to me, because folks, let me tell you… there ain't no wakeup call like the recovery room nurses slapping you awake twice in one day."

I'm too anxious even to chuckle.

He's leaving. No, he's staying. I don't know. Spit it out!

His hands are actually shaking on the microphone. I don't think I've ever seen that before—Carter's nerves actually rattled. Then, Carter clears his throat and looks right back at me, and his hands go still again.

"I'm retiring from the game. I'm coming home."

Holy shit. A hushed whisper sweeps the crowd at the same time as I think it.

My jaw drops, and tears flood my eyes.

"My doctors said I could get another season or two, maybe. But then maybe in five years' time, I couldn't walk. We all gotta choose what's important, right? You gave up other things you could have done to be here. I gave up sitting around eating cold cheese pizza for breakfast—best breakfast, right?" That gets him a little laugh, at least. "No? Come on, I haven't eaten carbs in four years!" he protests, and the second laugh is louder.

I can barely hear him over my thoughts.

He's staying.

"That's right," Carter smiles, and then he looks back at me. "I thought there was nothing I love more than the game. Turns out... we can't choose what we love. Or who."

Then he stops.

Everyone stops, waiting for him to talk.

But he's looking at me, and I can still read everything on his face.

Holy shit.

He's asking me for permission.

I wish I had a clipboard to clutch to my chest, because it's my turn for my hands to start shaking. I nod, hardly able to believe myself.

Carter clears his throat and looks at the crowd. "You know, there once were two boys who grew up right here, on this island. One of them..." He pulls a face. "One of them was kind of an idiot, actually." I laugh along with the crowd this time, even though my face is flushed and my heart is racing much too loud in my ears. "He went places because nobody ever told him he shouldn't be there, and he was too much of an idiot to notice if they did."

My laugh turns into an outright giggle.

He grins at me, relaxes a little, keeps talking. "The other was his total opposite. Way smarter, for a start. Real good at making a room of people comfortable—except he never realized he was the one doing it."

Oh. Oh, my God.

He *is* doing this.

I might faint. Or cry. Or both. Can I prepare myself to cry prettily, at least? I don't think so. It's gonna be big, ugly sobs.

"They both took a lot of knocks and tumbles in the world. And then they ran into each other—" he pauses and winks at me, and the islanders quietly chuckle as I blush. "And somehow, it made them change a little bit. The idiot realized that believing in himself too much wasn't such a good idea. He realized he could really hurt other people that way. Even people he believed in. People he... people he loved."

I've got tears fully dripping down my nose and off my chin now. Fuck. *Definitely* not pretty crying, then.

"And the smart cookie? He realized he had to believe in himself a little more. So, uh. Felix." The microphone in Carter's hands is shaking again. "I was that idiot, wasn't I?"

I try to laugh, but all I manage is a breathless little giggle. I raise my hand high enough for everyone to see, tip it back and forth in a, *Yeah, kinda,* motion, and I'm surprised at how much everyone laughs.

Even Carter.

He jams the mic in the stand and turns to grab my hands, and this time I feel the tremor running through them.

I squeeze as hard as I can, and he squeezes back as he swallows the giddy rush to his head.

"No rules," he whispers to me, his gaze flickering earnestly between my eyes. "Not anymore. Love doesn't play by the rules, does it? So why should we?"

I nod slowly, my eyes going wider and wider.

This is really happening. He's not just breaking the rules —he's pulverising them.

Carter grins at me, leans closer to the mic. "I love you,

Felix," he says, so everyone can hear. "And if you'll still have me… I want to be yours."

Not *him* having *me*, but me choosing him.

And I do.

Fuck. I always have, and I always will.

"Yes," I tell him, and he lets go of my hands to bend me backward.

Never in my life have I dreamed of being kissed like he kisses me now—hard and fast and *victorious*.

Until I'm just about falling off my feet, and then a little bit more.

When the applause finally dies down—and I realize it even happened, because I don't think I heard anything over my thunderous heartbeat—Carter grins.

"Now, may I entrust the rest of this wonderful event to the hardworking committee?" he asks Berty, who looks into the crowd.

I'm positive that's Marianne whooping and hollering back.

"I'll take that as a yes," Carter grins, and I cover my face as I laugh.

"Thank you all so much. I won't take any more of your time, folks. But please—come get some of this amazing cake —" he drops one of my hands to scoop up two slices, as I cover my face to hide my mixed laugh and groan.

Not even a plate? Or a fork? Come on! I have to set a good example!

But people are laughing, and Carter's grinning at me.

"—and enjoy the rest of your Strawberry Tea, and your time on Sunrise Island." He winks at them all, and then looks at me. "Trust me, it's true. You'll never be alone on Sunrise Island."

The applause follows us all the way to the parking area, before he looks down at the cake in his hands.

I laugh and let go of any sense of dignity as I grab one piece from his outstretched hand and shove it in my face, just as he does the same with the other.

"You've—you've got—" He bursts out laughing, spraying crumbs across the grass, and I laugh even harder. I can feel the cream and strawberry juice and everything, all over my face, and I don't care.

All that matters is my mile-wide grin.

He wipes his hands off on his trousers at last, then takes my arm again to lead me around the passenger side and open the door.

Oh, my God. It's another dream come true.

I've sat inside it, like most of the kids here have. But I was never one of the lucky ones who won the draw to ride inside it in the golf cart parade.

But things are different now. We're all grown up, and we're the stuff of some kids' dreams right now—getting to drive it on the most special of occasions.

I'm almost shaking as I slide inside.

"Actually," he pauses at the door just before he closes it, "do you want to drive her?"

I beam up at him, too happy for words. "That's so sweet. But, uh… I might faint."

He shakes his head. "Okay, I'll drive, as long as I don't have to brake suddenly." By the time he gets into the driver's side, I've decided not to ask any further questions about that. "And we'll both know that you're metaphorically the driver."

I can't stop my giggle. "Between us, we're just about a whole person, you know."

"Oh, I know." Carter looks at me as sincerely as anything,

until I almost cry again. Then he winks. "So, driver. Your place or mine?"

"Ours," I tell him, and I leave him to decide which that will be. All I want do is put my hand on his knee—all the way home.

CHAPTER Twenty-Seven

FELIX

We're naked before we even hit the bed, and somehow this feels brand-new.

It *is* the first time we've done this—at least, if we're heading where I'm almost certain we're headed. But I don't mean that. It's like this weight has lifted all of a sudden, now that we know those stupid rules are gone.

No more holding back from each other, and definitely no playing by others' rules. Just the two of us sharing this place we've made together in our hearts, for and with each other alone.

"Come here," Carter growls playfully, grabbing my thigh and wrestling me onto my back. I laugh, trying to scramble up the bed, but he's still goddamn strong.

"You won't even let me have a pillow?" I pout at him.

He grins at me, dark and hungry in a way that makes my already-semi turn into a full-fledged hard-on in a heartbeat. "I've waited much too long for you, Fox," he breathes out, dipping his head to kiss my chest and stomach. "And I'm hungry."

I gulp, and the thrill runs straight to my fingertips. "Yeah...?" I whisper, my thighs clenching unconsciously. "And what are you gonna do about it?"

Carter's grin gets wider. "I was hoping you'd ask that." Then he pauses and stares over my head for a moment. "Actually, I was hoping you'd answer that before I had to ask, because... I don't know how it works. Do you want me to fuck you, or do you want to fuck me, or do you want to swap, or...?"

I giggle and wrap my arms around his back. "Let me have a pillow and I'll talk," I negotiate, and he gasps.

"Whoa. You play innocent, but you drive a hard bargain. Fine. I'll meet your terms."

It's hard to squirm up the bed when I'm laughing like this, but it also makes my head spin with this unbelievable happiness.

I didn't know I could feel this much desire, let alone be able to laugh with my...

"Boyfriend?" I whisper aloud.

"Yes, boyfriend?" Carter answers.

I cover my face, but I can't quite hide the noise of happiness that slips out, and he grins at me so fondly.

"Just testing."

"Okay, boyfriend," Carter teases me. "Tell me everything."

"Say that with *a thousand times* more camp, and you'll be getting there," I smirk right back at him.

Carter tips his head back and laughs.

"But really," I add when he looks at me again, "I—I just want *you*. I want it all. So if you want to bottom for me sometime... you know, we can arrange that."

Carter grins at me. "And tonight, you're all mine? Just the way I told you I'd have you?"

I can't stop my little squirm, or the way my cock twitches. "Mmhmm," I manage.

He leans down to trace the tip of his tongue around my ear, and then kisses my jawline and mouths all the way down to my collarbone. "Good," he breathes out hoarsely. "Because I spent all week willing to give anything up..." he trails off, like he can't quite talk anymore, and I wrap my arms so tightly around him that *I* can barely breathe.

When he pulls away from me again, he leans in to rest his nose in the crook of my neck. "I have lube. I hear that's important, right?"

"I—yes, it is," I laugh. I'll never get over how he asks the simplest questions, but in the most unexpected ways. "Very."

"You have so much to teach me," Carter marvels, his eyes twinkling as he pulls the bottle onto the bed. "And I'm a *very* eager student."

I lick my lips, trying not to grind all over Carter's body. "Oh, I'll teach you as fast as you want to learn."

"And as hard?" he breathes out in my ear, and suddenly I'm breathless again. "As raw, and deep, and *wet* as I dream of?"

"*Yes*," I just about whimper, even though I don't think he's expecting me to answer.

Carter chuckles deeply. "Very good," he whispers, and then his wet fingertips are tracing around my hole, as his tongue learns the contours of my chest and the best way to flicker across my nipples so that I make sounds that I swear might break glass.

The first finger hurts a little, but he takes it slow—slower than I dared fantasize about. He kisses me that same way I fell for so hard and fast, like he wants to study my every reaction and memorize it.

Like he's planning how to put together his own playbook.

But if this is his starting point, I'm not complaining, because he's figured out a route *straight* to my dick.

"There's only one problem with us living together," he tells me as he slides his finger deep into me and back out again until I'm begging for another. "I won't be able to resist *this*. Every time I see you in the shower, I'm going to want to drag you right back into bed with me..."

A second finger slides inside, and heat explodes in my belly. I fight for breath, but then it eases and prickles and I'm suddenly hungry for more.

"And wrap you up in these blankets until just your cute little ass is sticking out, and take *full* advantage of you..."

It's everything I can do not to jerk myself off to his words. But I can't cum until he's inside me—and not just his fingers, I mean.

"God oh God oh fuck oh please—" I whimper, and he chuckles dirtily as he adds a third.

"And then," he whispers, "I'm going to put you back into the shower and talk to you about all the things I'll do next time, until you can't help but give me a show. You'll jerk off for me while I watch you, and when you cum, I'll be there to catch you."

This is why I'm in love with Carter Haywood.

Well, this and plenty of other reasons. But even in his fantasies, he's there at exactly the moment I need him most—and it's a moment I wouldn't have even thought about needing him.

I close my eyes, spreading my thighs wider.

"Please, Carter," I gasp, my breath ragged. "Now...?"

"Was that... *now*?" he teases. "Or later? I'm not sure I heard you."

My eyes fly open, hazy as they are, and I dig my nails into his thighs as I order him, "Right the fuck now."

He beams at me so happily that I can't help grinning back through this haze of pleasure.

Then his fingers pull out, leaving me achingly empty, and he soothes me with kisses on my shoulders...

And heat pushes against me, into me. Stretches me open, just like he promised, and glides deep inside me as I tremble and clutch onto him for dear life.

He's whispering into my ear, but it takes me a minute until my head stops spinning. I can't believe... I can't believe he's inside me.

And it's nothing like I ever imagined. Everything I ever dreamed of wanting seems so paltry in comparison to this.

Every warm breath on my cheek, every tender brush of his thumb on my hair... even the little cramps in my lower back as I arch desperately into him.

And more than anything, the love in his eyes when he looks down at me.

I never, ever dreamed of that.

As if he's reading my mind, Carter smiles until his whole face lights up.

"I love you," he breathes out, like he's still in awe of it himself, and I know exactly how he feels.

It's like seeing a perfect rainbow, or the perfect arrangement of tables at a wedding—but maybe that's just me. Something you wouldn't have imagined could exist, but when it's in front of your eyes and plain as day, you can't say it doesn't. All you can do is thank whatever forces in the universe brought you there at that moment to witness it, or —if you're as lucky as us, to be a part of it.

"I love you, too," I breathe out raggedly, and he bends his head to kiss me until I almost forget how to breathe.

The pressure inside me is shifting, the stinging fading away. Every time he moves his weight a little, it rubs against the spot inside me that sends another little shower of sparks shivering across my skin.

"I'm ready," I whisper.

Carter just beams at me. "Fox," he whispers, cupping my cheek. "My beautiful little Fox. You *are* ready."

I catch my breath, because that little touch of magic is back—like he's wishing something into being that I can't quite see yet.

But I think... somehow, I think it's *me*?

"Yes," I groan, rolling my head back as he pushes himself forward. He thrusts again, a little harder, and I moan even louder.

Within seconds, I'm not even doing it to encourage him, either. He's figured it out—the rhythm, the angle, all of it—on some kind of instinct alone, and all I can do is cling to him and enjoy the ride.

And boy, am I ever. I can't stop the noises spilling out of my mouth. My body is tightening up, my head spins with every thrust, and that's all before he starts to talk again.

"I've dreamed of this. Fuck, I've dreamed of having you like this. Under me, sweating and squirming and whimpering—"

"Nnh!" I throw my head back as sparks burst behind my eyelids. "Ah, *fuck*!"

I don't want to cum yet! But it's so hard not to when he's growling these things into my ear, his nails biting into my thighs, his weight pushing me into the bed...

And then he reaches down, one big palm gliding over my

cock before his fingers curl around my shaft, and I really *am* in heaven.

"Fuuuuck fuck fuck fuck fuck—"

"Oh, I will," he promises, and his teeth catch my neck in a sharp bite that makes white heat burst beneath my skin.

I gasp raggedly, clenching tight around him but desperate for him to do it again.

"I'll *have* you, Felix Harris, and I'll hold you against me, and I'll love you, and if you ever forget how much I love you…"

"I couldn't," I whisper breathlessly, but he just grins.

"I'll fuck it into you every morning and every night until you remember," he swears to me.

I clench harder around him, and he squeezes my cock harder, speeding up the pace of his wrist at the same time as his hips. "On second thoughts—nnh! I might—ah! Just forget… pretty frequen—frequent—frequent*ly*! Holy fuck! Carter…!"

The breathless, grunting laugh in my ear is the most gorgeous sound I've yet heard fall from his lips.

"Oh, Fox," he breathes out. "That's why I'm here. To remind you. Always, and forever, and *always*."

I'm trembling against him, arching against his body as I try desperately to hold out a little longer.

But I can't. The ecstasy is building up to a fever pitch under my skin, and whatever I do, I can't stop it. I don't even want to anymore, because I can feel the desperation in his thrusts, hear the raggedness to his gasps.

"Carter—!" I choke out, and I roll my head back as the final wave hits me.

He slams into me one last time before he grabs my hips, whispers my name in my ear, and buries himself so deep inside me to fill me with every fucking *drop* of that passion he promised me, and then some.

Only when Carter finally slides out of me does he finally let go to collapse next to me with a breathless moan. He sweeps me up in his arms and gathers me close, and I snuggle into the safe cocoon of his strong arms.

"I love you," Carter whispers into my hair, holding me like his most precious possession.

"Love you," I murmur sleepily into his chest, nuzzling as his chuckle thrums through my cheek. I let my eyes close, just a bit. For a moment. Maybe a little nap. It could be longer, but I don't mind that, either.

For today, neither of us have anywhere to be. We're just where we belong: right here, and together.

Epilogue
CARTER, SIX MONTHS LATER

I've been nervous for two solid weeks now.

Not because of Felix and Alph's whole family coming out for Christmas, and all the chaos that will come with it—though at least they have a whole house to take over, now that Felix really is living with me, officially.

But because of what else I have planned.

At one point, I was thinking about doing it on Christmas Day. Then Christmas Eve. Then the family trip got planned, and I thought maybe it was something I should do while it was just the two of us, because I sort of already did the public thing.

Not that Fox minds public things… my favourite, *favourite* little exhibitionist. But that's not what I'm trying to think about right now.

Point is, I have about twenty-four hours before his family arrives, and a ring I've been holding onto for… let's just admit to several weeks, and agree that "several" can cover a broad range, huh?

And with no romantic snowy morning in the forecast

EPILOGUE

now or for the next decade, and Sunrise Island's only restaurant booked solid for the whole month, it's kind of hard to engineer the perfect opportunity.

"Penny for your thoughts?" Fox teases me as we walk, hand-in-hand, around the island's shoreline.

It takes a couple of hours, so we don't get to do it every single day. He's too busy these days with his business—it's been taking off lately, so much that I think he's gonna have to hire someone else soon.

Goddamn. I'm so proud of him it hurts.

And we always try for at least half an hour's walk together on the beach. Even if we have to squeeze it in early in the morning, or late at night. *Other* things we squeeze in early in the morning include…

"Uh. Horny," is all I manage. A convenient excuse, and almost guaranteed to be true no matter what the occasion is.

Felix bursts out laughing. "I mean, when aren't you?" he grins at me.

Even though it's a crisp December morning, the sun rises here on the east side of the island, so it's surprisingly warm. I'm not surprised to hear other voices, or even the sound of someone playing Christmas music.

It might not be a sandy beach in the Caribbean, but it's *our* beach, and nobody's going to complain about a Christmas party.

Even when it turns out to be at Sunrise Brothers Cove.

"Whoa. What…?"

I blink two or three times, but the last thing I was expecting was…

Well, there's no other way of putting it.

My whole team is here.

Not *my* team anymore, I guess. Not technically. But the

EPILOGUE

guys who still live here—Vancouver, anyway—there's like fifteen of them, and they're all sitting around on the beach, drinking Coke and passing around bags of Doritos.

"Holy shit!"

"He's here!" someone yells as I let go of Fox's hand and break into a run, slamming into Levine to almost tackle him.

"Whoa! Dude, take it easy, old man—"

"Not old," I protest, putting him in a headlock. "Just injured." He squirms free and ruffles my hair, and then the rest of them arrive, nearly knocking me off my feet in the middle of the hug.

"Holy shit. Holy—It's—*all* of you."

"You didn't make it to this year's party," Scotty tells me with a grin. "Neither of you did. And we thought it was about time to meet this dream guy."

"He doesn't mean me," Zach pipes up, and I blink through the crowd. There they are—my other brothers, grinning back at me.

And, because I'm kind of an idiot, whatever Fox says, it only occurs to me now that this is a setup.

When I turn to stare at Fox, I stop dead and stare.

That's why everyone just started grinning.

Fox is kneeling by me, holding open a box with—it's—I can't believe it.

I honestly never saw this coming. I thought I'd be the one to propose, just because… I don't know why.

But all of a sudden, I'm really glad *he* did.

"Carter Haywood," Fox tells me, and his voice is so thick that my eyes go blurry right away. I clear my throat gruffly, but it doesn't help much. "You showed me that my heart was always mine—and then that it was always yours. You showed me who I can be. You showed me… that I belong."

EPILOGUE

I wipe my face a few more times, futile as it is.

"Will you marry me?"

It takes me a few moments to even get my voice back, and Fox just grins patiently up at me as he waits.

When I can finally speak, I let out a shaky breath. "Goddamn, Fox."

Everyone laughs.

"You're the driver. But damn, you can outdrive me."

"Despite first impressions," Drew shouts out, and Fox flips him off before I can, which makes me beam at him.

He really *is* getting there.

"Yes," I breathe out, because what else is there to say? "Yes, Fox. I really, *really* will."

He slides the ring onto my finger, and then he leaps on me and wraps his legs around my waist as I catch him and kiss him like *crazy*.

"Reach into my pocket."

"No," someone gasps, and the murmur spreads throughout… well, not all my friends. Some of them.

Okay. A few of them who didn't already know.

Fox looks at me, my pocket, and then me again. He reaches in, takes out the ring box, and then he starts to giggle.

"*No*."

I grin at him. "I sure hope that isn't a *no* no."

"No! I mean—yes! I mean—yes, I will, and no, it isn't—"

"If you let me put you down, we can clarify all of this," I grin at him, and he unwraps his legs in the most dignified fashion possible.

"Carry on," he orders me, and once I've caught my breath from laughing, I sink onto my knee and take the ring box from him. If we're going to do this, we're doing it by the rules just this once.

Because he deserves it—and so much more. He deserves it all.

"Yes," he whispers, before I've even got the box open. I laugh, but I stand up as I pry it open, and together we manage to get it onto his finger—between our kisses, and our friends' and brothers' cheering.

The rules were never really for us, were they?

Afterword

Dear reader,

Thank you for reading *Collide*, the first in my new Sunrise Island Brothers series! I owe so many thanks to so many people—for everything in the past few years, and for the many, many stories bubbling away once again.

I can't wait to share them all with you, beginning with the next book in this series: *Stranded*, available now.

Sign up to my newsletter at edaviesbooks.com/subscribe and you'll be the first to know about exciting news!

I also have a reader group, which you can find on Facebook at facebook.com/groups/edavies, to chat about your favorite parts of *Collide*, see cute bee photos and good news stories, and keep on top of my upcoming releases with a whole bunch of lovely readers.

Last but not least: always be you!

~Ed

About the Author

E. Davies grew up moving constantly, which taught him what people have in common, the ways relationships are formed, and the dangers of "miscellaneous" boxes. As a young gay author, Ed prefers to tell feel-good stories that are brimming with hope.

He writes full-time, goes on long nature walks, tries to fill his passport, drinks piña coladas on the beach, flees from cute guys, coos over fuzzy animals (especially bees), and is liable to tilt his head and click his tongue if you don't use your turn signal.

- facebook.com/edaviesbooks
- twitter.com/edaviesauthor
- instagram.com/thisboyisstrange
- bookbub.com/authors/e-davies

Also by E. Davies

Hart's Bay:

Hard Hart

Changed Hart

Wild Hart

Stolen Hart

Significant Brothers:

Splinter

Grasp

Slick

Trace

Clutch

Tremble

Riley Brothers:

Buzz

Clang

Swish

Crunch

Slam

Grind

Brooklyn Boys:

Electric Sunshine

Live Wire

Boiling Point

F-Word:

Flaunt

Freak

Faux

Forever

Freedom

After:

Afterburn

Afterglow

Aftermath

Rosavia Royals:

Barely Regal

Men of Hidden Creek:

Shelter

Adore

Miracle

Redemption

And more, including...

Sugar Topped (with Zach Jenkins)

Just a Summer Deal (with Zach Jenkins)

Limelight - Vino & Veritas, World of True North

Exposed - Dom Nation #1